BONES BOOK ONE

Crash Landing

by Jim Rudnick

ISBN-13: 978-1-988144-13-9
Copyright © 2016
Jim Rudnick

 **RUDNICK PRESS**

For my Susan...

Bones Book One: Crash Landing...

"As the first wisps of atmosphere touched the badly damaged explorer ship, the craft was on it's own AI—the pilot and nine of the ten occupants were already dead.

The only alive human lay in the robo-doc tank in the rear of the ship where he'd been for almost a full week. He had been injured during an asteroid incursion and had been placed in the robo-doc then. Now he lay half awake, half in a stupor, not knowing that the rest of the Drake's crew were probably dead.

Boathi sphere ships had come upon the Drake twenty light years out-wards, and had so severely damaged the ship, that even as the pilot lay dying and he kicked it into AI and called on full FTL, their fate looked sealed...

Inside the robo-doc tank, the surviving human lay in the liquid bath surrounding him, and he was still in that stupor of drugged medical aid. While he couldn't read it, on the interior visor, lay the dashboard with information for the patient—and it appeared he had still another two and a half days in here.

Alone...

Defenseless and in a sealed tank, as the AI would try to keep the robo-doc up and running to enable his recovery...at least that was it's next task..."

A Message to you from the Author...

  I just wanted to say thanks so so much for reading Book One of the Bones Series...

  As my Amazon bio says, being a youngster in the 1950's meant that I was a voracious reader in what has been called the Golden Age of Science Fiction. That meant that for me, my heroes were not on the hockey rink or gridiron - but instead in my local Library where at 12 I had a full Adult card (thanks Dad!) and took out more than 5 books a week.

  Everyone from Heinlein, Norton, Leiber, Pohl, Anderson, Simak, Asimov, Brackett, Gunn, Van Vogt and more....I fell in love with and eventually owned Ace Doubles of my own.

And while I never knew who wrote the Tom Corbett - Space Cadet series, I fell in love with them and they had a place of honor on my own bookcase too!

With that kind of an introduction to Science Fiction, it's no wonder that when I got my writing work done, I turned my own fictional side of my brain to writing same. It's one thing I know how to write - and a totally different matter to release same to the world - something that I've just started to work on....

Suffice it to say my own works are rooted in that Golden Age and it's that era that I'd like to one day be known as a teensy contributor to in some small way...

So once again, thanks for beginning my Bones series and wait'll you learn about the world that our hero lands on...

Enjoy and remember, in a series, characters develop and mature not the way we sometimes want...instead, it's like they have a life of their own!

Prologue ~

When the first wisps of atmosphere touched the badly damaged explorer ship and the craft was on its own AI, the pilot and nine of the ten occupants were already dead.

The only living human lay in the robo-doc tank in the rear of the ship where he'd been for almost a full week. He had been placed in the robo-doc after he was injured during an asteroid incursion. Now he lay half-awake, half in a stupor, knowing that the rest of the Drake's crew was probably dead.

Boathi sphere ships had come upon the Drake twenty light years outward and had severely damaged the ship. Even as the pilot lay dying, kicked the ship into AI, and called on full FTL, their fate looked sealed.

Now, those twenty lights gone, the AI had found a planet capable of life around a G-class star and was trying to get the Drake down in one piece. While the AI knew no one was left alive on the ship—except for the barely conscious human locked up in the robo-doc— the algorithms it ran on ignored that knowledge and focused on landing..

As the AI had been under full battle stations settings when they were attacked, those settings were not ignored. The Drake came straight down at more than Mach3—screams of wind pierced the interior as the Boathi attack had punctured the ship's hull. At less than a thousand feet, the AI tried to pull the Drake out of the dive and was only marginally successful as she plowed through a mile of tree foliage as the ship came level.

The AI was also set to find civilization, and as it scanned the large forest ahead, it detected a small set of foothills and some kind of infrastructure on the other side. Buildings, roads, and highways appeared to lie there, and the ship rose to soar above those hills. On a rough bank on the other side, AI cut power to the rear thrusters and tried to land on its tripod landing gear.

The fact that all of that was missing, as was most of the lower exterior of the hull itself, meant the ship simply fell the last twenty feet and lay canted off to one side but safely aground.

AI chimed and waited for a human to acknowledge the landing. AI chimed again. And again, but no one answered the chime.

The corpses of the pilot and co-pilot lay in their seats, and the chairs of the five scientists and two marines held corpses as well. All had been killed by the Boathi sphere ship as it had caught them coming up from a planet they'd just explored for the Empire. Nothing to report on that one, one marine had said just as the Boathi appeared off to port and the strafing projectile weapons riddled the Drake with holes. Not a big ship, the Explorer-class ship held fewer than a dozen crewmembers and had small sections devoted to labs and cargo space.. The robo-doc lay in the rear, however, out of the normal ebb and flow of the ship's traffic.

Inside the tank, the surviving human lay in the liquid bath surrounding him, and he was still in that stupor of drugged medical aid. While he couldn't read it, the dashboard on the interior visor showed patient information—and he had another two and a half days in the robo-doc.

Alone.

Defenseless and in a sealed tank, he lay, as the AI would try to keep the robo-doc up and running to enable his recovery...

CHAPTER ONE

Inside the robo-doc, the human dreamed. At least that's what everyone said—when you were under the robot's medical aid, time outside went on normally, but inside that tank and in one's brain, time was different. And dreams were common.

Javor dreamed. He dreamed of what it had felt like to cross the finish line in his first school race. To have beaten the other boys who had talked a good race, but who had never been out on the practice track like he had been. Rain, shine, and even hail once had not kept him from running those fifteen hundred meters over and over. Long strides. Pumping arms. Sweat running off his brow so thick that his shirt tails were soaked. But he ran. And on race day, he'd won. By quite a stretch, his coach had said, and in his dreams, he was now running once more in that same fifteen-hundred-meter race, but he was losing.

Someone was ahead of him by about a dozen yards as he realized this was the fourth lap of the track and the finish line was just ahead. He'd been tired from the one-hundred-ten-meter hurdles he'd finished just an hour ago. He'd thumped his knee on one of those wooden hurdles, and while it went down, he'd struggled to keep up and had come in second. So far today, he had a few firsts in the field events—javelin and discus, of course, and even a surprising long jump and the shot put too. He'd taken second in the hurdles and pole vault and third in the high jump, four-hundred-meter dash, and one-hundred-meter dash. It all came down to the fifteen hundred meters. If he could win it, he'd be the new decathlon champion of the planet, which would get him into the Empire games in a few months. In the Empire games, he would be able to challenge the best athlete from each of the one thousand planets that made up the Human Empire.

He half-smiled as he pumped his arms just a bit more, asked his thighs to loosen up a bit more, and asked his calves to tighten up a bit more on his strides. He closed on the man ahead of him.

Ten yards short.

Seven yards short.

Three yards short.

Veer outside just a little as the turn ended and the final straight lined up to the finish line.

One yard short.

Still one yard short, and his thighs started to scream at him.

Still one yard short, and his calves began to spasm at the end of each stride.

He knew he still had his kick, so with fifty yards left, he went into what little overdrive he still had.

Even.

He was even with his final competitor, and with every pounding step, he moved an inch ahead.

One inch.

Two inches.

Three inches.

And there was the tape … and … and he won!

He almost collapsed immediately and turned outward toward the massive stands full of screaming National Championship fans, and while he didn't go down, his calves were cramped up. He hobbled as others came up to congratulate him and tell him job well done.

He smiled in the tank. It was one of his biggest victories, and it floated above him like a cloud in a blue sky.

Yet somehow, he was no longer there at the big stadium but hovering above the asteroid that was the reason he was in the robo-doc. The *Drake* had received some scans that showed there was a deposit of Lawrencium close to the edge of the deep asteroid belt. She went in, and with the best pilot in the Empire Exploration section, he dodged and ducked and soared over asteroids that were as small as a flyer and as big as a lake.

The *Drake* was not what one would call an agile ship at two hundred feet long and bullet-shaped with arrays on the top and bottom sections of the hull. However, with a skilled pilot, she could be as agile as the pilot could be. The *Drake* had worked her way inward from the edge as the bridge view-screen scanners kept them aimed at the target asteroid.

It had been no one's mistake, Javor thought. At the same time as the *Drake* worked its way inward, something was hunting it from deeper within the asteroid belt. That something was a Boathi sphere ship, which jumped out from behind an exceptionally large asteroid and fired its projectile cannons full tilt into the *Drake*. This weapon sent out small, round drilling bullets like bearings that tore through the hull of any ship by the thousands. It made trying to seal hull breaches impossible due to the vast number of holes, and it used the vacuum of space to finish off anyone who'd been missed by the drilling bearings.

The *Drake* was no different. She was pierced

almost a thousand times as her klaxons went off. Eight of the ten crewmembers died from those bearings or shrapnel pieces of the hull. The pilot had about a minute to turn on the AI and set a course for anywhere twenty lights out, and as he hit the go button, he died of exposure to the vacuum.

Only one crewman was left—Javor, who'd been in the robo-doc now for a few days. It was trying to mend his broken arm and elbow and the abrasions on his left side he'd incurred on a fruitless away team mission on an asteroid just a few days back. Since he was in the robo-doc tank, submerged in the medical liquids, he'd missed the Boathi attack, and as none of those bearings had pierced the tank, he was still asleep.

And dreaming. And remembering.

Thoughts of the war that had lasted for more than one hundred years between the thousand-planets-strong Human Empire and the invading Boathi race, a race of reptilian aliens with a homeothermic metabolism and avian features, drifted through his mind. Like humans, they could easily adapt to almost any climate, which meant they could settle on all the worlds humans had settled on. The Boathi showed up with more than two hundred ships, without warning, at the edge of the Human Empire. They picked some planets to invade and sent down troops after seeding the planet with an airborne virus that killed 99.9 percent of the humans first.

A simple war, the humans had thought, for worlds.

Something they could deal with.

But talks had always failed.

The Boathi continued to take world after world. The ones they did not want were bombed with the airborne virus, and power generators, dams, nuclear facilities—anything humans used to generate power for their civilizations—were destroyed.

And they moved on. In those one hundred years, they'd taken at least two hundred Empire planets. While humans geared up for more and better ships to fight the Boathi, it had taken almost seventy years to get on an even footing, and the war was slowly now swinging in the humans' favor. The virus wasn't yet understood as the infected planets were now in Boathi territory.

A few Explorer ships had been selected to go back to the first fifty planets the Boathi had bombed and not bothered to invade or colonize. The mission was to check on them, find the virus, bring samples back to the Empire, and determine if the humans could recolonize them.

The *Drake* had been assigned to that mission. Their first stop was the virus-bombed planet

Artus4, off a sun about twenty lights farther into the Empire. The Lawrencium alerts had come from that system and its asteroid belt, and it had been luck alone that the pilot had lived long enough to engage the AI that had brought the *Drake* to this planet, wherever and whatever it was ...

#####

The *Drake* lay like a prize, its hull speckled with small holes. In the bright sunlight, it was beginning to smell with the noxious odor of decaying flesh and rotting bodies. That odor was like a magnet here as most food sources were few, and flesh was flesh to all scavengers. The river ahead of the *Drake*, on the other side of the road down at the bottom of the ridge, carried some of the smell away with its current and winds but not much.

Down under the *Drake*, as she sat listed to one side, small animals tried to climb up the narrow tree and shrub limbs to get to that smell. Most failed but some like smaller rats and a snake-like reptile were able to find purchase and get up and near the small holes in the hull. Some entered and slowly made their way to a corpse and began to eat. It was nature at its most basic tenets — what died became food for others.

The day after the crash-landing, more than a hundred of these scavengers got into the *Drake;*

others, bigger and less able to gain entrance, prowled outside. They watched each other as they hunted for access and often one fell to a larger predator.

Near dusk, a small group of humans appeared. They were aware of the ship because she lay in the bright sunshine high on the ridge above their town. They also could smell the stench of the corpses, and they were careful around the group of animals that such an odor attracted too.

One human put an arrow into a larger cat-like spotted hunter that sat in a tree above them, and as the body fell, it was pounced on by other smaller packs of animals. Large winged birds stood off to the side, watching and waiting to gain access to what was left.

But the humans stood still.

"It's a ship, all right," one said.

"A ship that looks like a human ship," another answered.

"But it's crashed. Surely no one could survive that as she plowed into the other side of the ridge first then ended up here," another said.

All nodded at that.

One human circled around and got beneath the rear cargo door, but it was too high.

"Can't get up there to try my handprint on the door lock," he said and shook his head.

Without recognizing who was at the door, all ships—this one most likely too—would refuse to open up a door to allow entry.

"Whomever sent this ship or what it means—'til we gain entry, it's all a mystery," the man with the bow said, and that got some nods of agreement, and he added, "We'll need some help here."

They left, going down the ridge quickly and back toward the town in the valley below by crossing the bridge a few hundred yards to the west.

As the sun set, the daytime predators dispersed, heading for their own lairs and dens, while in an hour or two, the nighttime ones slowly appeared, finding the odor of the flesh intoxicating.

A large carnivorous cat-like creature all in black took over the top of the *Drake*, lying on the ship itself, which kept the smaller predators at bay. The cat had no access inside the ship, but its presence made sure that no other creature would gain access either. It snoozed and snored on top of the ship, and it woke once or twice to growl and roar to make the smaller predators aware that it was in charge.

By dawn, the *Drake* was once again deserted and alone on the ridge. Inside, the devouring of the corpses continued, but that could not be stopped as the numbers of scavengers had increased.

The day progressed like the day before, and

nothing really changed. Instead of a group of humans visiting today, this time it was something else.

Dressed in torn and dirty clothing, two humans —or what had been humans—appeared on the ridge behind the *Drake*. As they made their way down the furrow that the ship had plowed, they didn't talk. Didn't communicate. Didn't stop from their direct line to the ship. Once they were below it, they tried to get up and into the ship. But they didn't seem to know about the airlock door—what it was nor how to open it.

They sniffed the odor of flesh, and nothing else seemed to matter.

They circled the ship a few times, looking for access, but not finding a wide-open doorway, they were unable to get to the cadavers that lay within.

As they circled, they were watched by a twosome of humans who had kept guard over the ship for the past two days.

As they circled around for the second time, one of those guarding humans nodded.

Arrows flew, and the two circling humans dropped, dying where they lay.

Two of the guards walked right up to them, and with what looked like heavy machetes, they chopped off the heads of the dying humans.

"Heads off is—" one said, as he wiped his bloody

19

machete on the grass to clean the blood away.

"Always good," answered the guard beside him.

"Smell will bring in more," the first one said.

"Yeah ... maybe we need to dig a pit—these two plus whatever died inside that ship. Will ask at end of our tour," the second one said, and they returned to sit below the ship, facing upward, and their attention was once again on the *Drake*.

As night fell, the twin moons came out as well. One was full and the other was a half moon, fully yellow and bright, and the nighttime sky was lit up brightly.

And once again, the switch over of daytime predators to nighttime ones occurred, and the guards switched out once too to sit and watch as the *Drake* lay still ...

#####

On day three, something happened on board the *Drake*.

Ding ...

Something was chiming for human attention, but it went unanswered.

Ding ...

It chimed again five minutes later and for a full hour, it chimed every five minutes.

And it was unanswered by anyone on the *Drake*.

Except the human who lay inside the chiming

robo-doc tank.

Javor knew that a robo-doc would chime every five minutes for an hour, and until then, it couldn't be opened from within. To further protect the patient, only the attending crew or medical staff could open it until that hour was up. After the hour, the screen display lit up the OPEN button, and Javor pushed it quickly. He noted on the display that his left arm and elbow were completely healed. The abrasions on his hip and thigh would be fine in two more days. "New grown skin takes a bit longer," he said to himself, and he slowly hoisted himself up onto one butt cheek and slid his right leg out of the tank.

His nose immediately reacted to the rotting flesh from the cockpit ahead, and he retched up what little he still had in his stomach right onto the deck. His bare foot was covered, and as he hoisted out his whole body, he had to walk in the slimy pool of vomit that lay to his right.

He carefully walked to his left and made his way to his bunk in the crew's quarters area. If he breathed out of his mouth, the smell subsided somewhat but not as much as he would have liked. Digging down into his top drawer he pulled out from under his bunk, he quickly grabbed a clean jumpsuit, socks, and underwear. It took a minute to clean his bare feet, and he struggled to get his socks on—time in a robo-doc robbed a patient of their flexibility for a few days after they said. And he agreed as he bent his leg even more to get that damn sock up and on.

He slowly rose and stood, leaning for a moment on the side stanchion of his bunk area—bunkie they called them on the *Drake*. Above him was the bunk for the marine sergeant, Nelson, and across from their bunk were the bunks for the other two marines, Binky and Fawcett. Both bunks were empty, and from what he could see, not a corner or an edge of the bedclothes was amiss. "Marines," he said to himself and then slowly moved up and toward the bridge area.

Passing through the next large area, the labs, was easy as he was able to use the edge of one of the stainless steel lab tables for support. To his unknowing eye, some things looked amiss, as there were several glass beakers and unknown lab items broken and piled up in corners. He raised an eyebrow at that and wondered, but he kept on sliding along the table as the AI recognized him entering the bridge. He choked and fell to his knees.

He retched again. And again as the smell and the sight of all of his crewmates' corpses lay in front of him.

Something was squirming under his knees, and he jumped to one side as a snake-like thing hissed at him. Around him were other scavengers, and on the corpses themselves, he could see their small bodies working away at devouring the bodies of his friends.

He looked up and screamed at the top of his lungs—not words but a scream that asked why …

And he vomited one more time, slowly standing and shuffling through the occasional rat or snake-like thing that lay between him and the pilot's seat and the *Drake's* dashboard. As he leaned down as far away from pilot Nancy Harvey as he could, he quickly saw that AI was on and engaged. He noted that it was set on Alpha1—the highest setting there was. Other variables could still be engaged, but the ship was protected as much as it could be even in the state that it was in.

He hit the view-screen display controls, and the whole front end of the bridge wall lit up with what lay ahead—the small town in the valley below. But in front of the *Drake*, about fifty feet away, a bunch of what he'd have to call un-humans was staring up at the ship. There were about twenty of them. They stood apart but were still a group, and everyone looked up at the ship.

Javor thought immediately of what vids called zombies—but that was unfair. If he was going to look at them using his explorer training, then his check box for them would be they looked plain bad.

Some had hair and others didn't; instead, their heads were covered with scabs and dried blood. Some wore clothing—most in fact—but that clothing hadn't seen a washing machine in years. Covered in dirt and stains, the shirts were as baggy as these people were gaunt. Thin. Un-shod too, he noticed with a couple that seemed to limp and had more mud on their legs than skin. Some were female and Javor really had to stare in a few cases to see what sex each was as he slowly scanned the group.

They stood as if they were on guard watching the ship. They did nothing but watch. A few tilted their heads back and seemed to sniff and sniff again. Javor was sure that the horrid odor in the ship could be smelled even at that distance.

He moved back and away from the dashboard and caught sight of himself in the mirror that hung on the airlock door.

Six feet tall. Two hundred and twenty pounds. Ex-decathlon champion. Ex-marine after only the mandatory two-year deployment, but he hated the discipline. Ex-entrepreneur but he ended up hating the restaurant business. Ex-college employee who loved to teach, but he hated bureaucracy. Ex-chef to a couple of Empire bigwigs, and now he was the engineer on the *Drake*.

Javor continued his self-assessment. Recently

healed broken left arm and elbow. Old ACL destruction on his right knee, which meant titanium inserts and that alien implant which gave him a great right knee. Old. More than fifty by a couple of years. Gray hair with the mandatory white goatee. Blue eyes. Crow's feet. Longish sideburns his sister said were his worst feature.

He knew it was time to open up. He had to get out of there, or he'd continue to toss his cookies, and there was little left to toss.

He looked at the AI panel, walked over to it, reached down, and made one change.

Vocals were now enabled, but he ensured it was only for his voice. He also added an override and used his birthday as the PIN. Long ago enough, he reasoned, that no one would guess that one.

He then said, "Open airlock," and on the side of the bridge, pointing partway toward the rest of the valley, the airlock panel slid open—as did the outer panel too.

He walked through the forward airlock in three steps and then stood in the open doorway and looked down the twenty feet toward the grouping of those un-humans. He checked and saw no weapons of any kind. In fact each was unadorned by anything other than the ragged clothing they wore.

All of them moved closer.

One or two, he noted, *licked their lips.*

More sniffed even more as the decaying flesh odor that was all around him poured out of the ship and down toward the town below.

Javor called out.

"Can you speak English?" He thought this was a great way to start.

Not a word came back as the group now stood below him, looking up, and he thought he heard small moans from them.

Javor considered that, and again, check boxes were checked.

Able to see that the Drake crashed. Check.

Able to see that help would be needed—if that was why they were here. Check.

Unable to talk. Check.

Unable to answer a direct question. Check.

Unable to do much more than, well, stare up at him. Check.

He wondered what would happen next as the group slowly grew larger and came closer.

Some came over the ridge behind the *Drake* while others seemed to appear from the town below too.

As Javor watched, one of the smaller un-humans, who had been leaning on a small sapling, suddenly tumbled over and fell in a heap. In a few seconds, a few of the ones around her were on top of her, biting and tearing the flesh from her body. In moments, she was not thrashing anymore. The group around her grew, and the sounds of tearing flesh and crunching bones reached Javor.

He flinched and felt that perhaps his first stab at naming these people un-humans had been too non-judgmental, too fair.

He was sure they were anything but human — *they were zombies.*

Flesh-eating zombies lived on this planet, and he'd just crash-landed on same.

He knew he'd again made a judgment, but as the feeding ones below finished up and looked up at him — their faces now covered with trails of blood and one holding an arm and gnawing on what was left of a hand — he was sure of one thing.

This was going to be an interesting planet.

But these things — zombies, he had to call them — ate flesh.

And behind him lay bodies. Bodies of crew mates — friends in fact. But bodies.

He shrugged. This would be an answer to one problem. But what other problems might it bring?

He shrugged again and realized that the next hour or two would be difficult.

As he jammed his foot against the inner deck plate on the airlock and pulled on the final corpse, he got an even bigger whiff of the stench and gagged once more. Fawcett was a big man and the two hundred and sixty pounds he was dragging was dead, dead weight. As he got the body to the edge of the airlock, he searched the pockets on the marine and threw everything he found into the same laundry hamper he'd found to hold the crew's personal effects.

When he tilted the body off the airlock, it fell and hit many of the zombies below that were still feeding on the preceding bodies he'd tilted out of the *Drake.*

The pack below had grown to more than a hundred now. They were all fighting to get to his dead crew mates, eating whatever they could bite, tearing flesh from bone, and even eating the weaker ones among them.

"Feeding frenzy for sure," Javor said to himself and looked past the furor below him and farther down the valley to the town itself.

Would have held more than ten thousand, he thought, in the old days. Wonder what she's down to now. As it was still afternoon, there were no lights to be seen, so he wondered about power. The Boathi had usually bombed all power plants— nuclear, solar, wind, and hydro—as well as dropping the virus, so it was possible this town had no power at all. Or maybe she did. He didn't know yet, and many more of his check boxes remained unchecked.

He looked down at the feeding below and noted that most of the bodies now had disappeared into the zombies as food. The word cannibal came to mind too, and as far as he knew, all zombies were cannibals. Least as far as the vids and the few books he'd read always said.

He half-smiled though as he realized that the zombies had handled one problem—the *Drake* was now not so encumbered with bodies and the stench of decaying flesh. He'd be cleaning up what was left inside, but for now, the zombies below stood and looked up at him. They growled and muttered among themselves, but it didn't matter—all of it was unintelligible..

The entryway to the *Drake*, via the airlock, was twenty feet above the zombies' heads and was the final limiting factor for his safety.

As he returned inside the *Drake*, he told AI to close up and seal the airlock, and the sound of those chimes meant that he was safe inside too. He asked AI if it could change the air completely throughout the ship at once for fresh, clean outdoor air and received a positive. Moments later, the smell was just about gone.

He asked AI if it could seal the various holes the Boathi projectile weapon had made. The AI responded, "Wait ... computing" and then responded in the affirmative. AI would have the exterior bots plug all the holes it could find and work on, but spaceflight might determine that some had been missed. It urged—as much as any AI could, Javor thought—that this issue should be considered before any attempt at leaving the planet it would be noted in the logs.

He went back to the cleaning station in the lab and found disinfectant, soap, hot, hot water, and cloths. He began the cleanup of the blood trails and body fluids that lay on the deck, the chairs, the dashboard, and the bench in the lab. He scrubbed. He washed. He sprayed the disinfectant and let it evaporate as it cleaned, and the *Drake* soon looked better.

Two hours later, the smell of decaying flesh was gone.

Bleach wasn't better but at least it meant that the Drake was now livable.

He listened to the scrape of the exterior bots as they moved around the hull, and he put it on screen to see what they were doing. Plugs of some kind of alloy were being inserted into the holes, which was then attached to some kind of an electrical cable attached to the bot. There was a flash, and that plug turned molten to fill the hole completely and provide an airtight plug to that hole. One more filled and the bot moved on.

Shouldn't take too long, Javor thought, and

suddenly he was hungry. He went back to the mess area and dug down in the freezer until he found some lamb. He liked lamb, so he put the MRE into the micro and said, "Start." The AI cooked the meal and chimed when it was ready. That gave Javor enough time to change—and to toss his dirty clothing into the disposal.

"*Laundry hamper,*" he said to himself, and he went back up to the cockpit to get the one that held his ex-crew mates' personal effects and hoisted it up onto the big table in the mess. He dumped it, spread out the items, and went through them one by one, as he chowed down on the lamb stew.

He drank water with it, but after a bit of math, he realized he had more than fifty dozen beers on board for him and him alone, which got a smile ... *that much beer could make for a great party—as long as he could find someone to share them with ... no zombies allowed ...*

As he woke from a deep and peaceful sleep, Javor slowly turned toward the open side of his bunk.

"AI," he said, "time—local time, please?"

"Seven hundred point twenty hours, Sir," AI answered.

Hmm ... Javor thought, *gotta fix that.*

31

"AI, my name is Javor—the *Drake* Engineer—so instead of using sir, can you please call me by name —and let's lessen off on name use too, shall we?" he commanded, and AI said, "Sure."

He got out of bed, took a shower, toweled himself dry, and dressed quickly.

In the mess, he grabbed a squeezable yogurt breakfast tube, and as he walked back up to the bridge, he thought about the planet and its past eight years.

If the Boathi had bombed the planet with their virus bombs, then most had died. From what he saw of the town below, it had experienced some destruction over those decades. So what was left besides the zombies whom he'd already met?

He sat in the co-pilot's seat, sucked on the tube of yogurt, and spoke to AI.

"AI," he said, "can you get Gallipedia up and running here?" He waited while AI seemed to work on this command.

"It is not possible to connect from here—there is no satellite linkage for the *Drake* to use. We do, however, have some archived materials available, Javor, as we assume you want to know more about this planet?" it said.

Javor nodded. Up on the huge view-screen, the Gallipedia logo appeared first, the silver wreath of laurels surrounding the big blue sun, and then the normal search function window came up, but a new screen that read Archive in the top left-hand corner quickly replaced it.

Beneath that header lay a system—this system, Javor assumed—as a G-class star shone in the middle of the screen. Eight planets surrounded the star, but the fourth one was circled in red for his attention. It also stated up in the top right corner that this information was now eighty-three years out of date. Something to remember, Javor thought.

On the screen, it was labeled Ceti4, which Javor presumed was its name before the Boathi had attacked.

What followed was a drill-down onto Ceti4 showing the various continents, oceans rivers, and lakes. Major cities were also marked. Down the sidebar on the view-screen monitor, the display listed that there was a planetary population of almost four billion people, human by race.. The major industries were agriculture, industrial mining and smelting, and advanced manufacturing of commercial goods. There was more information and it scrolled for quite a bit, but Javor had already stopped reading.

Four billion at a 99.9 percent death rate meant that about only four hundred thousand people had survived.

And if the zombies he'd already met up with

were four hundred thousand strong, he was in trouble.

He read a bit more, but there was nothing important enough to remember later.

Ceti4. Sounds like a great place to leave, speaking of which—

"AI. I want a full diagnostic done on our space-worthiness. All systems. All equipment. All with your best verdicts on what I will be able to count on. I want your full counsel on whether or not we can lift off, get up off planet, and go to FTL. I want it by end of today, got that?" Javor said, and AI responded, "Yes."

He smiled.

If he could get the Drake up and off planet and get to FTL, there was a way home. If not, the Ceti4 would be where this old guy would end his days.

"AI, any planetary citizens within, say, a mile of the *Drake* right now?"

AI computed and said, "Not a single entity at all, Javor."

He squeezed the last of the tube of yogurt into his mouth and threw it on the floor. Out from under the far wall, a bot appeared and slid over the smooth deck to the tube, which was quickly scooped up. It would be disposed of by AI sometime later, and the bot moved back under the wall sconce.

Javor grinned. That still worked.

He stood and as he thought about those zombies, he went to the small armory off the crew quarters. Once facing the door, he asked AI to open it and had to provide his birth date to get it to open.

"Six, thirteen, twenty-two forty-nine," he said, and the pocket door slid open.

Inside, the far wall was covered with mounted rifles, carbines, and shotguns of all types. Handguns sat on the wall to the left, and on the right were lesser weapons that had always been included—but some did make him wonder.

He took down one of his favorite shotguns, the combat twelve-gauge shotgun with its twenty-round magazine. He loaded the shotgun, took an extra full magazine of ammo, and then looked at the handguns. He liked automatics—Colts, if possible —so he chose a 9mm Colt Defender and took four magazines full of ammo for it.

He looked at the older weapons too. Bows and arrows. Lances. Spears. Bolos. Blowguns and darts. Slingshots even.

Not today, he thought, grabbed a hip holster for the Colt, and moved out of the armory, which closed behind him.

He smiled.

So armed, he could probably win any confrontation with a pack of zombies. So armed, he'd go into that town below.

He went over to one of the equipment lockers and found the rope ladder, which he would need to reach the ground twenty feet below the ship's outer airlock door.

He walked through the bridge one more time and requested that AI open the inner and outer airlock doors. Javor hooked up the collapsible ladder and made sure—doubly sure—that the ends located within the airlock were on the rollers provided.

He asked AI to unroll the ladder and down it went. He asked AI to roll it up and close the outer airlock door. AI did that too.

Should be good, he thought as he had AI unlock the outer door and roll down the ladder again. He slowly climbed down the rungs.

Once on the ground, he realized his boots were now covered in what was the few remains of his crew mates, and he swept his boots off on the free grass a couple of feet away. He looked right, then left, and down the valley too. Not a single soul, or zombie or whatever they were, was around.

He looked up under the *Drake* too. One of the bots had twisted around some kind of tree root and was still using its skills to fill holes, and Javor nodded to himself. Not many more. He wandered almost half the length of the *Drake* and saw that all the landing gear stanchions were gone. Not there.

Missing. The *Drake* was lucky she sat on top of so many trees and shrubs even though she listed to one side. But without the tripod landing stanchions, the *Drake* would need to lift off with a degree of speed so she would not fall first. He shook his head. Engineer, sure, but pilot ... not so much.

He went back to the ladder and looked up at the open airlock door.

"AI, up ladder, and close and lock the outside airlock door," he said, and AI complied perfectly.

He turned, looked down the slope, and grinned.

Time to get that right knee a-going. He slowly worked his way down the ridge line. He crossed some wood lots, then a few glades, and even some cleared land. There was no agriculture, but some kind of land management had been in effect.

He slid the shotgun off his shoulder, clipped it to his brown belt that crossed his chest, and wondered how long it'd take to aim and fire. Didn't need to aim, he thought, as the shotgun would clean out an alley as usual.

He made sure the Colt at his side was also easy to access, and he drew it a couple of times to make sure.

He walked down the last part of the ridge where it met a small park, and he went out onto the street and looked in all directions. One way, down toward what looked like downtown, some cars were parked along one side of the street, and all the windows had been broken out. Beyond the cars, the street, which had garbage all over the asphalt, slowly turned to the left, and he saw a set of streetlights. Burned out. Not a shining light. Power not on for the streetlights at least.

He turned one hundred and eighty degrees and looked up the street that curled to the right. No cars were parked there, but there was a bus—a big orange bus—that had been burned and lay on its side. Beyond the bus, on the side of the street that faced the ridge, were small stores and shops. Each one had been damaged and maybe looted. Signs were so badly darkened that he couldn't make out what they might have once said.

Javor turned to face the closest side street and had to move slightly down the street to be able to see it fully. Ahead of him, the street was empty, but the shells of various stores and patio restaurants lined one side. Tables were turned over, chairs were missing legs, garbage was everywhere, and broken glass from smashed windows littered the ground.

In front of one of the farthest patios, smoke drifted up from within what looked like large oil drums.

"Where there was smoke, and there was smoke right there," Javor said to himself, *"there had to be someone who started that fire."*

He half-grinned as he made a mental assessment that one of those zombies he'd met yesterday couldn't have started a fire.

No way. Too much skill needed. That made him a bit happier. Another check box on the zombies was checked off.

He made sure to stay in the middle of the street to keep away from any kind of a trap or ambush, and he walked slowly toward those oil drums.

As he approached, he saw a piece of an awning on the street, and he went around it, not really knowing why. But he went on. As he got closer, he noted there were some signs too that had been torn down, and he was glad to see they used galactic English. He smiled as he went by what was once a store that advertised that they'd never close. He wondered what time they'd be opening today.

A bit farther, he slid the safety off the shotgun and put his trigger finger alongside the trigger shield, ready to fire if need be.

He reached the first of the drums and looked inside. It was a simple fire of pieces of wood, and some was unburned which meant that someone was tending these drums.

He walked another half block farther to the first intersection and stopped in the center.

Behind him lay the burning drums and the street that would lead back up to the *Drake*.

Ahead, the street curved now to the left, and it too was full of shops and wrecked cars.

He looked left and saw that the cross street had a solid wall of a warehouse with a series of docks where trucks could back up to take on goods or deliver them. One truck was still there, but its trailer end was ripped open, and Javor could see garbage inside.

He moved along a bit and got past the warehouse. He had no idea why he'd chosen this way, but ahead there was a lineup of more than a half dozen oil drums, all smoking profusely.

He walked carefully still along the middle of the street, and when he was close to the line of drums, he went up on the sidewalk and moved closer. Along one side lay a long wooden ladder, and beside it two corpses, which he knew were zombies. Dead. Not moving which was a good thing.

As he walked over the top of another of those canvas awning remnants, it caved in on him, and he fell backward into the black hole as his shotgun went off loudly. He hit his head and fell unconscious …

CHAPTER TWO

Finn moved the map just so. Making things easier for Vera and the rest of the Circle was what he did best. A smile crossed his thin and narrow face as he looked around the meeting room.

Map with latest intel. Check.

Refreshments—just coffee this time but freshly brewed, and there was real milk for it too. Check.

While tablets were still at a premium, there were notepads and pens ready too in case someone wanted to take notes. Someone other than Maeve who always asked why she was the only one taking notes.

He looked over at the private. Wait. One stripe. Was that a private or a corporal? As long as the young man stood at attention at his post in the doorway alcove, he really didn't have to know more.

The walls were still holding the latest in the Regime's current missions and what success had been as yet reached with most of them. He glanced at the closest wall and noted that the tablet recovery mission over in Crandon, the large port city that lay to the southeast of Arlington, was as yet still open. It wasn't the manufacturing center for the old tablet business company, but the enormous port that was used to ship out—and in—goods like the tablets that were still so very dear. Paperwork from eight years ago could still be trusted, and more than five containers had laid dockside in Crandon on the day the Boathi had attacked.

Five full containers of tablets—needing new batteries for sure—but that kind of swag was well worth the ten-man team sent to the port to see what they could find.

Not that it—as Finn looked up and down the listings—*was the only mission that was important.*

But tablets would sure help.

He looked at his watch. Ten minutes until the Circle meeting was scheduled to start, and so he went and got a fresh coffee—with milk—and loved the unaccustomed smoothness of the rich flavor. Milk had been a recent addition as the ability to add power to the pasteurization line over on the farms had been on the books for years, and it had just been done in the last two weeks.

"*Power. Power is so bloody important,*" he said to himself, "*that it meant more to the Regime than all the tablets and milk combined.*"

He sniffed his coffee. No milk smell but then he guessed that the fresh coffee smell would eradicate what little fresh milk might add. Since the coffee itself was a complete chemical surrogate, perhaps it would always drown out all other smells.

As he took another sip, two women appeared at the door, and after the guard checked them off his list, they entered.

Maeve, of course, went straight to the pile of notepads, and taking one, she glanced at Harper, the other woman.

"Harper, you'll need one of these, correct?" she questioned, but her tone was more like an order.

"Not in the least, Maeve—you keep the records and logs, and that's good enough for me," she said as she grinned at Finn and helped herself to a coffee.

Maeve shook her head. "Eight years of no AI, no records, no logs, and the folks in charge are too lazy to write down what they do—that I just can't understand," she said, and she clicked the pen a couple of times to ensure that the tip went in and out.

Finn smiled. "Maeve, please take two if you'd

like," and that got him what he thought was the evil eye from Maeve as Vera, Nixon and Reid, the last of the Circle, entered the meeting room..

Vera nodded to the guard who left the room and closed the door behind him. "Okay, please get a coffee and then let's get started," she said, as she poured a cup of coffee.

Sitting at the head of the table, she looked at them all and said point blank, "We have intel on an incoming ship, correct?" and she turned to Nixon who nodded and pointed at the map that lay on the table.

"Correct, Vera. About four days ago, a ship— unknown as to any details on it but still a ship— flew at better than Mach3 through some of the lands west of us and then crash-landed, as far as we know, near the town of Maxwell," he said and all nodded. That had been known now for days.

"Power grid control noted this, as the ship screamed through our atmosphere, but again all it can tell is that yup, something flew by. We have no records—not that we even have the equipment to be able to detect same—of what kind of ship it is. Boathi? Empire? Someone else? We just don't know," he said as he paused.

"But as you know, in Maxwell, we do have a small cadre of followers there. All they can tell us so far from their high-freq Yasu base station is that the ship crashed into a ridge, tore off much of its understructure, and is lying there in disrepair. Seems too," Nixon added, "that the stench of rotting flesh—corpses—is pouring out of her too. They wonder if anything could have survived the crash, and their noses tell them probably not."

That got them all talking at once, and after letting it go on for about a minute, Vera smacked her hand down on the tabletop hard.

"Okay, there's lots we don't know. First thing, exactly how far away is this Maxwell?"

Finn spoke up first. Details were his strength.

"If you use the most straightforward path—across the Badlands to the old power plant at the Adair Dam, then west via the old interstate highway—it'd be like 225 or so miles. While that way is fraught with both dumb and smart zombies and sects, the normal pace of ten miles a day would mean we could have a team there by the end of the month. Safer way is instead almost due east from Arlington, via the Long Gap through the Gray Forest and then south along the ridge highway system. Less bad guys, less danger, but about twice as long to get there," he said. He knew which he'd pick if Vera called for a vote, but he had no idea what was coming next.

"Nixon—can we ask our local cadre to investigate more fully? Go and knock on the ship's door, so to speak. If anyone is left alive inside, surely the fact that a local with a hunting rifle is a lot less to fear especially as they're a space-faring lot would make a difference?" she wondered.

Nixon nodded. "Yes, I can ask. We can't order but the offer of a few hundred rounds of ammo generally gets the job done," he said.

Vera nodded. "Okay, we wait 'til we hear more. Next," she said as she sipped her coffee.

Finn nodded.

Maeve would record this and pass it along to the Circle log keepers. He'd add it to the board with the note that more intel was needed, and the Circle moved on to the next item.

As his head began to throb, Javor realized with a start that he'd just fallen into a pit that had been covered with a phony awning tarp.

"Trap," he said to himself, *"I've just been trapped. Where the hell is my shotgun?"*

He felt around and found his shotgun still attached via the lanyard to his vest. His shotgun had gone off when he fell, and that was surely enough to bring along his captors.

"Audit time," he said to himself, as he slowly rose up on a hip and looked around. The tarp about fifteen feet above him let in some light, and he

wasn't sure he liked that. Three bodies—three almost totally eaten bodies—lay near him, their corpses dried out and looking long dead.

The body of a dog or something like a dog was tucked over near one side of the pit. A faint growl sounded, and he assumed the dog was growling at him.

Maybe not, he thought as he slowly rose against one wall of dirt and tubing. He flicked on the light that would shine off his left shoulder and said, "Max bright" at the same time.

The dog appeared unable to back away much, but it tried and hid in the niche behind it.

There were five corpses and he noted that one of them still had an oozing blood trail from a calf and that would mean he was a recent pit capture. He saw nothing else. No ladder up, no rope even—no way up and out.

He had about forty feet of a simple arlon rope with him. If he could grab something up top and use his leverage, he might be able to get up and out.

He took one more audit of the pit and its occupants. He moved slowly out and away from the wall. From his vest top pocket, he pulled out a jerky bar, unwrapped it, and then took a bite. He chewed very loudly and noisily for the effect, and then he slowly tossed the remaining half toward the dog who had eyes for nothing else.

In less than a second, the dog jerked out of his overhang little niche, grabbed the bar, and had it gone before he turned and was back in that niche, licking his chops.

The dog was about a third of his height weighed about one hundred pounds, and had big teeth, but he had much need of grooming. His fur was torn and there was blood splatter on one flank too. Yet he moved quickly and had favored no limb, so he appeared to be healthy—just not a human eater, Javor hoped.

He said, "Good boy," slowly dropped his shotgun, which had been trained on the dog the entire time, and twisted the strap of his backpack around so he could get to his rope.

As he was struggling with the clasp, a voice sounded above. A human female voice, in galaxy English too.

"Are you okay?" she asked.

And as surprised as he was, he answered automatically, "Yes but pissed off," and he heard a chuckle.

"Wait, ladder coming down," she answered, and sure enough that partially broken ladder appeared over the top of the pit and angled its way down to rest on the pit bottom.

As he watched the ladder slowly arc down, he realized that dog was now standing right at his side watching too. It had come out of its niche and looked like it wanted out too.

He thought about that for a second as he cursed his stupidity for even trying, but he dropped a hand onto the top of its head and scratched.

The dog angled its head to one side to increase the scratching pressure on an itch perhaps, and Javor knew he was a human dog and not a feral one. At least so far. He adjusted the ladder to be less truly vertical.

As he got ready to come up the ladder, he said, "There's two of us—me and my dog, and we're coming up backwards." He reached down to pet the dog once more. He positioned himself with his rear end tucked into the bottom rung of the ladder. He used one more jerky bar to gain the trust he needed as he slowly wrapped both arms around the dog and gently stood up and leaned backward.

Holding the dog gently as the dog chewed, he slowly raised one foot to the bottom rung and pushed up, his body lying on the rungs above. One by one, he slowly mounted the ladder backward.

Why am I taking the damn dog? I haven't owned a dog in forty years.

This one he somehow knew was different, and living in a pit, eating whatever fell in and died was one thing that Javor could not fathom for anyone— or any dog.

At the top, a woman of about twenty-five stood pointing her old-time rifle at him from across the pit. She knew not to get too close which showed some tactical knowledge.

He rolled onto the street at the edge of the pit, and the dog squirmed out of his arms.

And was gone. Off down the street lickety-split and never even looked back.

Javor grunted and looked over at the woman first and then around himself.

Behind one of the oil drums still burning was a man who must have thought he was hidden, but he was easily seen, Javor thought.

Up on the roof above him and behind his back sat another, one that Javor could not see, but he was reflected in the partial window across the street.

Tactically, these guys need help, he thought, as he stood up tall and let his shotgun lie untouched on his chest.

"Thanks for the help up and outta that pit. I'm sorry to say that I didn't even see it coming," he said, and his voice was full of embarrassment.

"Dumb zombie trap. Thing is, they forget about it, and then whatever falls in, dies. Still get eaten, of course, but you'd think if you ran a trap, you'd check every day, right?" the woman said, her aim still centered on his chest.

"And why did you check?" he asked.

"Heard that shotgun blast—not something we hear much anymore. So had to come to investigate. And we found you. Judging from you and your weapons, you're not from Maxwell, are you?" she said.

He looked over at the man still trying to hide behind the smoking oil drum and said, "If you and your friend up on the roof want to join us, we can all talk—this is a long story," and that seemed to surprise the woman.

But she nodded and the oil drum man, who looked to be about forty, joined them, and moments later the rooftop sniper did too.

Javor sat down, right there.

He smiled at the woman and spoke to her. While the story was not short, he took almost a half hour to explain who he was, where he was from, about the Boathi attack, the Drake AI finding Ceti4, and then the last few days from the robo-doc sleep through to the opening up of the Drake and his first encounter with zombies.

"At least that's what I called them—so did you too, right? Zombies?" he queried, trying to learn as much about this enemy as he could.

The woman nodded but the oil drum man spoke up instead.

"Two kinds of zombies. One kind we call dumb zombies—who used this pit for instance to trap unsuspecting folks—even though Maxwell doesn't have many. Not too strong IQ-wise, pretty much just an eating machine. You can kill them easy and yes, they do stay dead—"

The woman interrupted. "But then there's the smart zombies—they don't look the same but again are driven to eat. They do have some kind of IQ though as they can think, plan, and attack too. They too will eat their enemies, but what is more scary is that if you get bitten by one—and saliva is passed into your bloodstream in less than a day—yup, you're a brand new smart zombie. That and you can't really kill one of the smart ones. They rise right back up within minutes. Unless you cut off their whole head. Headless bodies can't be controlled, and the heads die in hours. Remember —a headless zombie is a good zombie. It's what we teach our kids," she finished off.

"And yet, from what I've gathered, you three aren't zombies—dumb or smart. So who are you guys?" he said, as he looked at all three of them.

"Ahh, history lesson coming up," the woman said, and she lowered her rifle until it pointed down at the ground.

"And I've just decided that you're not going to be an enemy of the Regime either. Let's go, shall we— oh, we'll take you to our local cadre headquarters. You can meet the chief, and get the history lesson then. Personally, I've got that T-shirt, so let's get going," she said.

As she hoisted the rifle onto her shoulders, she looked at the other two and said, "This guy is okay, no need to keep him under guard," and that seemed to do it as they all shouldered their arms.

Walking farther up that same street, an alley appeared on the left, and the woman took point, readied her rifle, and walked carefully down the center of the fairly narrow alley.

Along one edge sat some unused garbage cans as the garbage lay thick around them. Above them on a rickety looking fire escape, a corpse that was more bones and skeleton sat tucked into a corner of the metal structure.

As they walked a full block, across two more streets, and then veered off on a tangent to the side, Javor noted that everything looked beaten up, unusable and unkempt. The colors on everything from old tattered signs to official notices on buildings or storefronts were long out of their best look. Washed away, tired even, was how he saw things.

Once down a side street, he looked and saw a freshly painted storefront. He was about to ask about it when the sniper guy beside him shook his head and said, "Don't ask—it'll come later," and they continued to move toward what Javor thought would be the center of town.

At a side street branching off to the left sat a few more burning and smoking oil drums, and yes, this time a piece of brown tarpaulin was cozied up right next to them.

The woman pointed and said, "Another sewer pit, dumb zombies too … so avoid it," and they went on toward their goal, wherever they were aimed.

At the next larger intersection, where there were streetlights that had once worked and a few cars and trucks that were burned hulks from their showroom days, sat that dog.

He looked at them as his head and forelegs tried to dig into the asphalt and his hindquarters stayed erect.

That used to signify let's play, Javor thought, as he stopped to watch what might happen.

The woman held up her hand and they all stopped.

Javor wanted to know why the dog was there in the middle of the street and seemingly just watching them.

He walked out a bit toward the dog and smiled at him. He smiled just enough to show interest. He reached slowly into his top vest pocket, opened up another jerky bar, ate a small bite noisily, and then tossed the big part toward the dog.

The dog leapt for that treat and chomped it down quickly. Javor saw that it still was hungry as most dogs always were.

He reached into that pocket again, and keeping his hand in the pocket, he walked up slowly to the dog who sat attentively waiting.

Reaching the dog, he pulled out his last bar, and peeling back the plastic packaging, he offered it to the dog who took it nicely and then chowed down on same.

He petted the dog cautiously on the head as it chewed and then noticed something he'd not noticed before—cadaver smell.

He half-turned, said, "Cover me," and then stepped around the dog to look inside the closest car.

All he saw was burned interior. In two more cars, one lying on its roof, he saw the same.

When he reached the delivery truck, also on its side, he had to squat to peer in through the still glassed in window. Inside was a body wearing some kind of a military outfit. Dead though. From what, he couldn't tell, but suddenly the dog was beside him and whining.

"Sorry, fellow, nothing I can do for him—or her. But you're still fine, boy," he said and slowly stood up. The only way into the truck was up the side to the top where the driver's side door would be.

"Probably open," Javor said to himself, "but still the guy is dead."

He turned to the oil drum man and said, "If you're able to get up and get into this truck, there's a fresh body there in some kind of military camo outfit—and they have a backpack too. I'd say the intel would be worth the effort—but then I'm not in charge of this cadre."

The woman nodded her assent, and the young oil drum man hoisted himself up and into the truck.

The dog, of course, paid attention but did nothing but sit at Javor's side at the front of the truck, watching.

Moments later, the oil drum man was out and handed the backpack to the woman.

"Would like to know what's in that later—but could you tell how the guy died?" Javor asked.

"Yup, he took a slug to the chest. Big slug—single shot probably as he was getting outta the truck. Moved his dog out first, went back for gear, and BAM—dead," he said.

He'd assumed, as Javor had too, that the dead guy was the dog's owner.

"And while I'm not in charge of this cadre—is he wearing a type of uniform that you know? I mean, do we know who this guy is?"

That got a simple shake of the head and the woman interrupted.

"And yes, I am in charge of this cadre—so let's get back to base, shall we? If the dog follows you, that's okay by us too, mister." She turned away from the pile of vehicles to move alongside the park that lay at the center of Maxwell and down a side street. Javor read the name of that side street off the tired sign, and it was Bixby Street.

After ten paces, Javor looked back to see the dog casting glances at the truck, then at him, and then back at the truck.

"Always good to have an ally with ten times the smell ability and night vision," he said to himself, and thanked that explorer class on local fauna from a few years back as he whistled sharply.

Behind him, the dog's head whipped around, and his feet were quickly trotting toward them as they moved down the street.

One on my side, Javor thought, as he scratched the offered head, and they walked down the street together…

Bixby … the dog would be named Bixby …

At the end of the industrial park, where fallen buildings and railway tracks with burned boxcars stood, one building was not so much in disrepair. Windows still had glass in them, or rather, most of them did. In front where the offices had once been, the overgrown shrubbery and trees draped themselves across the front of the building. The overgrowth didn't hide it so much as give it the look of being long forgotten.

At the building's side, a row of loading docks was all empty except for a couple that had old trailers still in the docks, but the trailers were empty, of course. Around the back, the steps from the big employee parking lot were clear all the way up to the rear fire escape too. At the top level of the three-story building sat a guard who was enjoying the afternoon sunshine but still remembering to scan the lot below.

"No strangers," the guard said to himself for the hundredth time today and reached back into his inner vest pocket for another sweet. Someone had discovered a cache of candy—hundreds of pounds—in a locked truck over at the railway station, and he'd been given a handful. He had idea what kind of candy it was, but it had sweet chocolate and some kind of goo. "Goo was sweet too," he said to himself, and he looked down below again.

No strangers.

Not five minutes later, the door to the metal walkway opened up and someone came out.

It was Andrew.

Andrew was his replacement on guard duty.

He slowly wedged his foot under him and stood,

passing the rifle to Andrew as he did.

"No strangers, Andrew. Not a one," he said, and Andrew nodded as he slowly sank down to take the still warm seat tucked in the corner of the metal walkway that led to the stairs down to the ground.

"Bye, Ralph," he said, and then he looked down to the huge parking lot.

Ralph went down the walkway to the door and then went through into the third floor of the building.

Inside, he hung up his windbreaker and then went down the short corridor to the next door and through same to report.

Moving along the wide hallway, he nodded to some others as they looked at him, and he eventually made his way to the big room that held his bosses. He knocked on the door, heard "enter, and did just that.

Inside, there were three people sitting at the large table that papers were spread out on. He went over to speak the woman, who he knew was called Jane.

"No strangers, Jane. Not a one," he said and waited.

"How many seagulls today?" the man across the table asked. A snicker followed the question.

Jane looked up at Ralph and smiled as she shook her head. "Ignore William, Ralph. Good to see your guard duty went well. We will see you tomorrow at the same time."

Ralph left the room.

"William, making fun of Ralph—or of all of our somewhat challenged citizens—is a side of you that I don't like," she said dryly.

"Then let's pass a law for us that no one can bite a zombie. When you do that, you get Ralphs or Andrews ... not a brain between the two of them. I've been saying that now for years," he said as he shook his head.

While the three of them at the table—Jane, William, and Roger—were the head of this group of smart zombies with now more than a hundred citizens, there were truly few of them that were not challenged.

Roger nodded. "Yes, that does make sense, 'til you remember that someone has to guard the building, trundle out of town for food from the farmers, go to town to check the traps—items that I'd never do. Nor for that matter, I'd think, any of us would do," he said, trying to put an end to the argument.

Jane nodded. "There's what—twenty of us and that's fine. When we need new citizens, we simply bite a zombie, clean them up, and teach them a few words and a job. Works and has worked since bombing day. Now," she said, "back to this crashed ship."

She turned and looked at a couple of photographs they'd had taken on the day after it had landed. One showed the Drake, lying canted on one side, on the ridge above the town to the west.

"We know that there was at least one survivor—because he tossed out all the crew corpses, which our local Maxwell zombies devoured pretty quickly. We also know that the Regime cadre was seen dropping by to watch too. We also know that we cannot gain access—it's twenty feet up and the front airlock door is solid. If the ship has an AI, it does not respond to a simple open as we've tried."

She looked over at William. "Ideas here? I would think that if this is human—then we want them to join us—not the Regime. If this is Boathi, then we want them dead. Agreed?"

That got two nods from the others and a lull in the conversation too.

"Then until we learn more—like when the survivors come out and look around—then I say we put the ship on hold and proceed with our plan to ambush the cadre. Can we at least continue with that plan?"

Again, there were nods around the table. She pushed the map of Maxwell to lie in front of the three of them and began.

They worked on the rationale behind motivating

the cadre to all come at once—to an event they would need to orchestrate well. They had more than enough smarter citizens to be able to over-run any kind of resistance, as long as they could control the location. They knew that once captured, the cadre would be bitten and infected with the virus that each of them carried, and their citizens would grow in number. Not knowing how many cadre members there were in total was somewhat worrisome—but for the past year, they'd only seen seven different faces. Seven they could handle, so seven was what they planned on.

Roger smiled. "An event big enough for the whole cadre to show up—do we still have that old ordnance from the Maxwell Armory in storage? I mean those big howitzer shells?" he said as he laid out a plan with an opening salvo that could not be ignored.

#####

Where the park ended, the river moved toward the center of town. Downtown it would have once been called, but now it really looked like it was down. Buildings were torn away sometimes with only a shell of I-beams and hanging drywall being seen. Others had tumbled down onto their foundations with bricks and slabs of flooring lying right out into the street. One building, Javor saw, must have been leveled completely as it was now a pile of rubble a hundred feet high with not a single floor remaining up. Still more were just windowless shells, the piles of glass shards deep near the overhang of rubble.

Bixby, Javor noted, *walked well around such shards, which spoke of a dog who'd learned from experience. Again, good to know.*

They moved again down the street and then along the edge of the river.

"This river—goes where exactly, as it appears we're heading upstream," Javor said, noting the eddies along the close shoreline.

The woman answered, "Runs from the mountains about three hundred miles upstream, past Maxwell for another seventy miles to the sea. Southern sea we call it—but it's a part of the Racine Ocean too." Her tone said don't ask for any more info, so Javor nodded and shut up.

As they walked, he noted that the town was quiet. No urban noise at all. Not a car or bus or train or plane made a glimmer of sound, so that'd mean there were none of those available for human use. More check boxes to fill. He couldn't help being an explorer, but where and when he'd file this report might not ever occur.

As the small group wound around a roundabout with a couple of distressed cars, Javor saw a nice-looking building right ahead. It was made of some kind of white stone, but whatever it was, it shone nicely in the sunlight. In front of it was landscaping that had long ago gone wild but still gave the building some kind of uppity status, he thought, so he asked about it. "Is that the cadre home turf?"

The woman grunted as she stepped over the remains of a burned telephone pole and went through the small hedge at the edge of the property. Javor followed and noted that Bixby came along too. He seemed even to know where a shortcut was as he bounded ahead, and he reached the front portico of the building before the humans did, sat, and waited.

The woman and the oil drum man followed, and Javor came up last. The sniper man had disappeared, and Javor raised an eyebrow at that.

"Rescuing you took Bruce away from his post up top. Best shot on Bones for sure," she said.

He stopped her as they were just about to enter the building's front door.

"Bones? This planet was called Ceti4 in Gallipedia—has there been a name change?" he asked.

She nodded to explain.

"Not officially—but all of us down here on Ceti4 have taken to calling our world Bones—like a skeleton, eh? Boathi bombs on our power plants and the virus they unleashed on the people have left just the skeleton of Ceti4—hence Bones ... easier to say too, eh?" she added and then opened up the front door but held out a hand to stop him.

"Wait," she said. "We have pretty dumb AI here, but it's gotta find you, scan you, and then ask for your okays ... just stand still." she said "AI login." out loud.

Ahead of him in the large foyer of the three-story building, a bot sat dead ahead. From the large machine, a beam of green lanced out to look at the woman first, and across the bot's screen, flashing lights flickered—all turning green.

The green beam moved to him, Javor realized, and those lights flashed and flashed some red colors too—and then the bot's klaxon sounded loudly.

The woman quickly said, "AlphaControl— execute stop order nine dash T sixty-six," and the green beam snapped off and the bot seemed to go to sleep.

"You're human, right?" she asked. "As the AI found something it didn't like," she added.

He tilted his head to her and then smiled.

"Was an athlete like forty years ago—blew out my complete right knee. It's been rebuilt with alien technology and tissue—two or three times as strong as a human knee. But yes, I have had some issues with security scans since then. Could you have your

AI re-look at me and somehow ignore the knee?" he asked, and she nodded.

She walked right up to the large machine, made a couple of passes on the keyboard, and then said, "Stand still" once more.

He did just that, and once again, the green scan beam looked him over from head to toe; lights flashed and then the bot seemed to be satisfied, as it said in a mechanical voice, "Authorized, subject will be noted as B thirteen. Please use that code to login in future," and then the green beam switched off.

He would have to remember that login ID, but he was glad that he'd passed. Of course, three shells from his shotgun would have also gotten him into the building too, but that was another story.

"Upstairs—let's grab a bite and we can chat there," the woman said, and she took the stairs two at a time, while Javor followed her with the oil drum man.

In a small anteroom, the two cadre members divested themselves of their vest armor, weapons, and extra ammo packs. Oil drum man also tucked away a couple of throwing knives into a cubby, and Javor put his shotgun down on a side bench. The Colt he'd keep on his hip, which he thought was prudent, no matter what kind of sideways glance that got him from the woman.

She also took a moment in front of the long

mirror to comb out her hair and use a wet-nap to clean her brow for a moment and then grinned at him.

"This way—Jimmy is on lunch duty today, so it's gonna be good," she said and led the way out of the anteroom to a larger area that would have once been called the mezzanine, as it looked down on the big foyer below.

From a large table against the wall, another man nodded to him as the woman pushed Javor to be first in the lineup for food. He handed Javor a plate, piled already with a good-smelling stew, added a big chunk of fresh bread, and then pointed to the silverware and napkins.

"Sorry, as usual, 'til we get over to Lindos for more spices, we've got no hot sauce at all," he said apologetically.

Javor nodded. The stew smelled so good he was sure he didn't need anything extra.

He took a seat at the large round table, ensuring that here he could see the foyer and the stairs if not the actual doorway outside and the doorway to his right to the anteroom too. Tactical, still, he thought. He noted that Bixby had also climbed the stairs and now sat with his side against the mezzanine bannister's down to the foyer.

The woman joined him with twice the amount of stew on her plate and a bottle of water as well, something he'd missed, but a quick nod to oil drum man who looked at him at that instant got him one too.

The three of them sat. When Jimmy joined them, the woman talked, mouth full at times, as she began to polish off the mountain of food in front of her.

"You know the history, right? Eight years ago, the Boathi dropped hundreds of bombs on our power plants, dropped virus bombs, and the NEMPS that they detonated killed all of Ceti4's— Bones'—electronics. All of them. We now have what we've taken those eight years to re-learn and re-manufacture," she said as she dipped a torn corner of that fresh bread into the stew and slopped up a whole mouthful at once.

"Since then, society has reconfigured itself. Virus killed like 99.9 percent of us—the ones that didn't die split into a couple of camps—sects or cults, I'd guess. Some of us are fine—like the Regime and our cadre. Not many of us though—say like ten percent of the total Bones population. The rest the virus didn't kill, but it made them kill and eat flesh —kill anyone, even each other if they can and eat each other too. If a zombie—and yes, I hate that word too, bites you—you're a zombie. Takes a couple of days for the virus to totally infect you, but you become one of what we call the dumb zombies, can't talk, can't reason ... only kill and eat." She took another large bite of bread and stew. She guzzled down a half bottle of water to wash that away, tucked the heel of her hand into her chest to force back a belch, and continued.

"However, sometimes—and we've no idea why this happens—a smart zombie is created. Still can talk, reason, still wants to kill, mind you, but eats food same as us. They're smart—smart as us. That was one of their traps you were in—but here in Maxwell at least, there's so few of them that they can't do much really. They do fill their ranks by bringing a few of the dumb zombies into their group with a bite—does make the dumb ones a bit smarter but not so much as we'd notice," she said toying with her water bottle.

"Your shotgun told us something was amiss hence our double-time to that trap, and I doubt that they've even sent anyone to look into that. So we found you. And that's us ..." she said as if to quit with her tales.

"Not quite—mind telling me who you all are," Javor said as he spooned another good-tasting mouthful into his mouth.

"Sorry, sure—I'm Sue Fines—leader of the Maxwell cadre group. Sniper up top right now is Bruce Ridgeway, best shot on Bones. This here is Wayne Barker, who you met at the trap, and our cook today—we take turns, eh—is Jimmy Bellanie.

Great stew, Jimmy," she added as she was now wiping up all the dregs of the stew off her plate. Only one not here is Rick Parkin—he's off hunting somewheres—he too is a great shot, in the woods, I mean."

Javor looked at her and then down to the remains of his plate of stew.

"So with various factions—what'd you call them, sects, I think, all at war, how do you feed and look after yourselves? School for the kids—though I've not seen a single one as yet? Society? Culture? Travel? And yes, power? How did that stew get cooked today?" he asked.

Wayne answered since Sue's mouth was full of the remnants of her bread and stew.

"Food is a cooperative mostly. We suspend our adversarial tendencies to shop at the farmer's co-op, and that goes for the cadre and the smart zombies only here in Maxwell. Dumb zombies eat each other—wish they'd hurry up," he added.

"Those power-destroying bombs all those years ago did do something to the climate too—we get bad, bad storms sometimes. Our northern latitudes have a climate that is much colder than it used to be too, we're told. And oh, if you ever hear of a nor'wester, meaning a storm coming from the northwest, then you'd better batten down the hatches, 'cause they're always real doozies," Jimmy added.

"After a decade or so, the farmers gathered and become pretty important for all of Bones—and we all learned to treat them like a neutral in our own lives. Power is different though, but again it's like the folks who now provide power—and that's a whole other story as to who can get power and at what costs—do so but you apply. You pay and no there's no money on Bones either—you pay with what you get asked to supply. Then there's the Slavers—those who capture and enslave folks to sell them to the farmers or to the power apostles too, but not many of them around here. Free cities too, like Lindos, are popular as within same all have access to buy and sell whatever one might want. Not as safe as we'd like, but still Bones exists," he said.

"And then along comes a spaceship," Sue said, and that brought them all up to Javor's story, and that was where he'd have to think on it for a bit. And he said so.

"Lots here to digest—and before I tell you my story, I will need rest," he said, as he stood up and looked around.

"Down there, last doorway on the left has a great couch—you and your dog will be fine in same, and yes, the door will lock," Sue said as she burped this time right out loud.

He grinned at her, complimented Jimmy with great lunch, and ambled off after giving Bixby a whistle.

Together they entered what must have at one time been a private office. He closed and locked the door behind him too. The only other door went to a bathroom, so he took over the couch, and Bixby came over to lie at his side. His hand fell off to pet the dog who lay still, and soon both were asleep. Their first full day on Bones came to a close.

The Boathi captain was livid, his green scaly skin almost glowing with indignation.

"Explain yourself, Sub-alternate, and you'd better be correct," he said to a cowering crewman on the bridge.

The *Sophon* had been scouring this system—all three planets within the Goldilocks zone—for two whole days and had not a single thing to show for all that work.

"Captain—my apologies, but I was only going by our records—which are already some years out of date," he answered, his mouth tight as his green scales on his upper lip area were as tight as could be.

He bowed even lower and then slowly raised his eyes to stare at his captain, who snorted at him in rebuke.

"Only some years is an excuse, Sub-alternate. We were here back then. We audited these three worlds and decided that they did not fit within our expansion plans so they were left for the bombing sphere ships to deal with. Records show what exactly, Sub-alternate?"

The underling nodded as his tongue flicked in and out of his reptilian-shaped mouth.

"Sir, yes—there were over two hundred of the Empire's power stations destroyed—and each of the three planets was also virus-bombed as well. By the time our forces moved on, we had killed almost everything on the three planets, Sir," he added.

The captain turned back to his view-screen on the far wall of the *Sophon's* bridge and pointed.

"And does that look like a world that is dead to you, sub-alternate?" he said ironically.

Below, as the *Sophon* was hiding just off the edge of the planet's smaller moon, the sidebar of the view-screen reported much traffic, up to a space station in low orbit. On the planet itself, as the terminator was about halfway across the globe, one could see large well-lit cities and towns—something that could not occur if the planet had been made incapable of power production.

"So either the records are wrong—or the view-screen is wrong—are those my two choices?" the captain said, as he pushed back into his seat, his scaled hide scraping along the seat's upholstery.

The sub-alternate hated to add something else, but he knew he had to offer up one alternative, no matter what it might cost him. So he spoke up a final time.

"Sir, one other way to look at this—perhaps the people of this planet have rebuilt and repopulated their worlds quicker than we would ever expect. Sir. Perhaps, Sir," he said, and his bow became deeper as he now stared down at the bridge deck.

That got him no response. Well, not a verbal one. He had kept his eyes were closed, and the trembling in his leg was making his robe flap.

He waited. Nothing.

He rose a bit. Nothing.

He finally opened his eyes, and the captain was staring at the view-screen quietly.

"Thank you, Sub-alternate, for your candor. Could have had your egg dissected, so I know the risk that you took with this far fetched idea. I don't know what to believe here—I doubt seriously that the records were doctored—in other words, I believe that yes, we did kill 99.9 percent of each of these three worlds. Yet this one, and we note only this one, is back with system ships, power, cities, and almost where we found them those decades ago."

He scratched the edge of one of his eye socket rims, where the smaller scales on a Boathi's face met the larger scales on the side of the head, and his finger claw made a rasping sound. Boathi were notoriously itchy—it was as if the scales that covered their body just did not do well on a sphere ship. Yes, the temperature was maintained at a crisp fifty-nine degrees Celsius, and yes, there was always a directed breeze at them by the ship's AI, but all they truly wished for was to be off ship, back in the cool jungles of their home world. But it was not to be.

The scratching rasp ended and the captain leaned over to his alternate.

"Do we have any means to end civilization on this planet? Big enough bombs or even quantity of same?" he asked, but he knew the answer.

"Sir, no, Sir. We are a raider ship—enabled with the tools to fight a space battle or raid outposts. We have little in the way of bombs, and all are smaller than would be needed to even flatten one of those human towns. Never mind a city. And as we know that these humans have system-capable ships, we are also in a degree of jeopardy too. We must maintain silence and hide 'til we leave—we suspect that they do not have FTL as yet—but that can't be far behind, Sir. They did have it, the records show, so it is on their list for future development—I am hoping that they're slower at that than rebuilding their world, Sir," he added with a hint of irony too.

The captain seemed to digest that and then nodded.

"Mark the records well then, Sub-alternate," he said "and note their level of achievement. Send that by Ansible marked INCOMING INTEL to the Empire section. Take deep scans as well and add them—all the intel we can send will help. Search grid, please," he said, and on screen the planet below disappeared and a grid of lines appeared on a star chart.

"Sub-alternate, you can update, please," he said, and the rasp of a claw on a scale on the back of one of his hands could now be heard.

"Sir, yes—the ship we are searching for—this *Drake* explorer ship—punched out in FTL for twenty light years only from where we found them in the asteroid field," he explained.

On screen, an amber circle appeared around nine stars from the center of that chart, the asteroid field.

"We have now searched for them within three systems, and they are not to be found as yet. We have"—a small red circle appeared around the remaining five systems that all lay within those twenty light years—"only five more to look at. We will find them, Sir," the sub-alternate said, and he meant it.

On screen, the red circle with the five systems in it was expanded, and one of those systems was a double star too.

"Let's try the double next," the captain said and nodded to the sub-alternate to engage as the sphere ship jumped to FTL and was gone.

CHAPTER THREE

"Easy, take it easy," Roger said, as he walked carefully down the exact center of the street. Ahead of him were three of those pseudo-smart zombies—the ones that he thought were a complete waste of a bite. They seemed to not understand that being close to something that sat at the side of the street might mean it was hiding something that might want to hurt you. But then again, as he knew, these zombies knew no fear. Eat or be eaten was their mantra—and even biting one to increase their mental abilities didn't seem to fix some of their habits.

He forgot about them as they rounded the corner, and ahead sat those six smoking oil drums and the hole in the street too. No awning cover so he imagined it had gone in when some—*hey, wait a minute. The ladder was inside the pit. Someone had helped out someone else,* he thought .

Up at the edge, he peered over and saw just the three bodies from before. Nothing else.

He looked at one of those other zombies and said, "Andrew—climb down and bring up those bodies. No eating either 'til the pit is empty—and don't forget the awning cover either."

Andrew scurried to comply. Up and down he went, carrying first one and then the other two bodies up and out of the pit.

Roger asked, "Are you sure that there were no other bodies down there?"

Andrew and the other zombie were staring at the bodies. Not much there for a meal, Roger thought, but then he didn't think they cared.

"No one else—no other bodies," Andrew said as his hands went out to the closest body.

Roger turned away as the two ate; watching jaws and teeth rip into a calf or tear a lip away from a face was not something he enjoyed watching, and he waited until the two had gorged themselves.

"Put the remains into one of the drums—along with more wood," he said, and the two tried to do that as best they could. Once, a piece of wood wouldn't fit so well, so the zombie put it back and got another piece.

"Ahh ..." Roger said to himself, *"some kind of brain*

79

power does exist," and he chuckled.

He waved them away, went over to the drums, and took out some accelerant from his backpack. He stood well back and squirted a healthy dose into all three of the oil drums that held a body, and the fires within surged up, smoke billowing.

He nodded. Good. That'll clean out this pit.

He went back to lay out the awning cover remnant as the cover to the pit's entrance, having to move one of the oil drums on top to hold down an edge too.

Pit is reset. Don't know why as all we ever catch is zombies, but that's what we do.

With his twosome of dumb-now-smarter zombies as company, they retired down the street to return to their industrial park headquarters.

#####

He woke with a start. Bixby was the culprit.

He sat staring at Javor, whining a bit, and Javor knew why—*outside for a pee,* he believed.

He checked his Colt—still there. He put on his boots and slowly stood and stretched. The ceiling here was at least fifteen feet above his head, so he crouched down a bit, and using his right leg only, he suddenly jumped and touched the rough popcorn texture of same. Fifteen's about average, he thought, knowing he could touch almost twenty feet too. Alien tissue is a wonderful thing. He grimaced as he really would have liked to have stayed one hundred percent human, but the doctors had done what doctors do.

He went to the door, unlocked it, noted the loud noise it made, and went down the mezzanine floor to the set of eating tables. Judging by the shadows, he'd been asleep almost five hours. It was now late afternoon and he smelled the freshly brewing coffee and went down the stairs to the foyer below. Bixby came along too, and he went through the doors now, ignoring the AI bot behind him, and let the dog out onto the front portico.

Must have been some kind of headquarters for something long ago. Right now, Bixby was out there treating the grounds like his own personal toilet. My how things change.

He whistled and Bixby's ears came up. He looked like what a police dog he had seen fifty years ago, he thought. But Bixby didn't turn his head. His attention was out on the street.

Nothing there. Could see not a soul, no noise, nothing.

Of course, a dog had a much better sense of hearing and smell than a human did. So Bixby could hear something he couldn't.

He whistled once more and the dog turned and came right to him. He smiled as he rubbed Bixby's head and murmured, "Good boy, good boy" a couple of times.

Back inside, the green scanning beam lanced out at him, then the dog, and then turned off.

Guess we're family, he thought, and he moved back up the stairs to that coffee. He stopped to go through his backpack for a couple of those jerky bars and fed Bixby first.

Moments later, Sue came out of another room well down the floor and across the mezzanine. She nodded as she got coffee and sat with him. She said nothing, sipped her coffee, and looked out the windows across the mezzanine at the leaves on the trees just outside the building.

"Was the Maxwell Courthouse a long time ago, and I like the fact that we took it over," she said as if to answer his unasked question about the building.

"Been here, I think, what, four years now, and with the AI bot, we're pretty protected. Long as we've got power and ammo, that is," she added with a half-smile to him.

He nodded and said, "Time to talk?"

Sue nodded.

He explained. He didn't go into much history but did say that with the Empire's advances in tech over the past decade, they were slowly winning the war with the Boathi. He told her a half-dozen

Explorer ships like the Drake had been outfitted with the latest tech and manned with an odd-ball selection of marines and scientists—and him too for some reason he didn't know. They had been ambushed about twenty lights outward by a Boathi sphere ship and had jumped to FTL under full AI as the crew died.

"I was already tucked into the robo-doc, so I missed it all, but all nine of my crew mates were killed. Came out of the robo-doc just two days ago and had one hell of a mess to clean up," he said and took a big sip of the coffee.

Would love some cream. But all they had was some kind of white powder—artificial milk, maybe—and so he'd taken it black with three sugars.

She grinned at him and said, "And as I think I know, the robos are always tucked away somewhere off the main flow of any ship—probably saved your life!"

He nodded. "Right—most likely—but here's the thing. I am no pilot—FTL-wise, I mean, but if I can get the Drake up and into the atmosphere here on Bones, I can get around the planet if needed. Diagnostics are going on right now, and I've my doubts as the Boathi used those screw bearing bullets to pierce the hull hundreds of times—no way to know what else they cut into or destroyed. But if the Drake has to sit above Maxwell, then so be it. She's got more'n fifty years of power left, full AI, full defensive measures ... if I was a hermit, I'd just close the airlock and not even bother to look out the view-screens."

He noted that Bixby was looking for more food and pointed to him. "Know things here are tight, food-wise at least, but is there something I can trade or buy from you for the dog?" he asked.

She turned to look at Bixby, grinned, and then nodded. Getting up, she went off the mezzanine, and he heard her steps down to the ground floor and then a minute later coming back up.

In her arms, she held a big box—maybe thirty kilos—but she was a strong woman, and she dropped it on the floor beside him.

"We got this, what, a year ago or so? Anyways, it's dog food. We did try to bake some with some of it, and William says he likes it in his yogurt—not that we get much yogurt anymore. But sure—it's yours—for a price. I'd very much like to see the *Drake*—inside, I mean, and look at what's the latest tech too. Deal?" she asked and held out her hand.

He shook it quickly and then went over to the long side table to find a plate and some kind of scoop. No scoops and human plates only. He took an orange one—the only orange one—and went back to sit down beside her again.

"Orange plate is mine then," he said, and he

quickly drew a knife from a hidden scabbard alongside his left calf and cut a hand-sized hole in the top of the bag. He added four big handfuls to the orange plate, picked up the plate, and laid it off to one side.

Bixby did not follow with anything but his eyes—until Javor whistled and said, "Eat boy." In seconds, Bixby was halfway through the pile of kibble. A minute was all it took, and by then, Javor had found an old bowl that he filled with clean potable water and placed it beside the now empty dish so Bixby could have a drink.

He returned to sit beside Sue and smiled. "Thanks ... the dog is important to me," he said as a way of trying to get her to understand.

She nodded but tilted her head to one side. "Course, something that's important to someone can be used against them too—just saying," she said, and he filed that away for later thought.

"So, Bones. Sounds like I'm going to need to talk to someone—whomever runs the planet—about the *Drake*. Would that, in your opinion, be this Regime you're a part of," he asked, but he already knew her answer.

She grinned. "Absolutely correct—that's who you need to see. And if the *Drake* ain't gonna fly, it's like 250 or so miles as a hike. Through some treacherous country, through some bad sects, through a power city, and then a whole set of worse areas we just call the Badlands. All that way to Arlington, where the Regime is."

He thought about that for a moment or two as Bixby came over to lie beside him.

"Any way to talk to them—the Regime, I mean—before I take such a hike? Or maybe they'd like to come here instead?"

She shook her head. "Not a chance of them coming here—the seat of their government is the town of Arlington, so you'd need to go there to see them. But yes, we do have a working ham radio setup, and yes, I can connect you with someone there so that you can make up your own mind on taking that trip. Hell of a trip too, eh!" she said as she shook her head negatively.

He thought on that for a moment as his hand dropped onto the top of Bixby's head and he scratched. The dog tilted his head for more pressure on a certain spot, Javor smiled.

"Okay, here's what I need to do. Go back to the *Drake*—yes, you're invited for a look-see tour and see what the diagnostics have shown as her space-worthiness. Or just flying ability maybe. Once I know that, I can then speak to this Regime with more intel and be able to come to some kind of an answer for my future here—and theirs too," he said, and that made the best sense.

She looked at him and said quietly, "Are you at all concerned that these Boathi—the ones that attacked you—might be following your trail?"

It was a question that he'd pondered a few times in the past few days and one that he had no answer for yet.

He shook his head though as he was sure he shouldn't be quite so open with her about this.

"Not really. We jumped twenty lights as I said and here in the old Empire worlds, taken over or bombed by the Boathi that could be like dozens of various systems. I don't think that they're that interested in us specifically. Not enough to try to find us like a needle in a haystack type of scenario," he said.

His voice sounded sure about that and all he wanted was to be right. There was no real way of knowing though and he shrugged at her.

"So we go on, like Bones is the only world we gotta worry about, right?" he said.

She smiled and rose at the same time. "I've got rounds—wanna come for a quick tour of the courthouse grounds and all? Once I mark it as okay, AI takes over 'til breakfast tomorrow—fresh eggs I hear too," she said with a grin on her face.

He nodded and went to fetch his shotgun. He put on his armor vest first and then the gun into the shoulder belt clip for safety and he was ready. Javor and Bixby joined her down in the foyer for a walk around the large old mansion as dusk fell slowly on Maxwell.

#####

Javor moved slowly along the final street that led to the bridge over to the ridge line where the *Drake* still sat alone. He looked left and then right and then watched Bixby who was ahead of the three of them. The dog didn't vary in his path at all. He went straight up the final few yards of the street and then to the bridge that went off to his left.

Bixby turned around, sat, and looked at Javor as if to say that everything up to here was fine.

And it was, Javor noted, and he, Sue, and Jimmy all moved with a bit more purpose to the bridge.

"River is low it looks like," Javor said.

"Normal run-off in the spring gets her up, yeah," Jimmy said, "but now as the summer gets started, she drops. Will go down at least a couple more feet by fall too." He pointed out to the close shoreline.

Javor stared at the rocks and the muddy banks. He wondered *if there were fish in the river or some kind of weasel or marten or mink that might live there. There was no way to tell,* but he knew a great recipe for weasel that he'd tried often before.

What, a hundred years ago, he thought and smiled.

"Okay, let's move out," he said.

Sue let him take control as they had moved through Maxwell so far under her watch. He took point—or rather, he followed Bixby who took point —and then went across the bridge, skirting the burned cars and the bus that was on its side. Not too close, he thought but then he realized that if Bixby walked a foot away from something, there was nothing on the other side to worry about. Good to have a dog, he thought and thanked the zombies for the pit that had brought them together.

Ahead, Bixby waited at the edge of the bridge as the road stretched out in both directions and followed the meandering ridge line above. Javor tossed his head to the left, and Bixby got up out of his sitting pose and trotted down the street toward the *Drake* which lay above.

In less than two hundred yards, they were directly below the *Drake*, and Javor whistled as he came to a stop. Bixby trotted back to him to sit at his side. He looked up at the underside of his ship and waited until the other two were with him.

"There she is—the *Drake*. Almost two hundred feet long, mostly labs and cargo holds and living space too. Robo-doc in case it's needed. More than, I think, like fifty years of reserve power, great leading edge AI too. Could call it home happily, but in this case, we gotta see if she can fly. Let's go up,"

He moved to stand below the front airlock door. "AI—Javor here, acknowledge," he said, and the AI chimed three times.

"Open front airlock door and drop ladder," he said next.

The airlock door slid open, and a collapsible ladder suddenly dropped down out of same.

He looked at Bixby.

"You'll come up later, boy," he said as he climbed the ladder first and was followed by Sue and Jimmy.

Moments later, another airlock port opened up beside the open door, and a small lift slid out of the horizontal opening. Javor took the step over to same, and then he aligned it with the airlock itself and said, "Down."

And down it went. Bixby was cautious but eventually moved onto the lift deck. Javor said "Up," and up they went.

Once they were all inside, Javor said, "AI, button her up, please," and there was some noise as the lift and ladder were retracted and the doors sealed up.

"Nice AI," Sue said.

Javor nodded and went over to the co-pilot's seat to sit, and his guests found the bench against the close wall to their liking. Bixby wanted to explore, so Javor said, "AI, my dog is named Bixby—please allow him full access to all the ship—but do not allow any auto-doors to equipment or storage to open for him. Got it?" he asked, and the three chimes that answered meant yes in AI speak.

He looked at the dashboard, specifically at the monitor, and said, "AI, diagnostics to date, please, up on the view-screen."

As he said that, a whole series of icons and flashing lights appeared—most he noted in red and only a couple in green.

"Shit," he said, and he meant it.

AI had run most of the diagnostics, and so far, all had shown that the *Drake*—while habitable—would never fly in space again. Too many of the Boathi screw-bullet bearings had pierced too many of the systems that were needed to go to space.

FTL was gone.

Inertial drive was iffy—AI couldn't tell until she was up and in the air, which was bad because if she couldn't fly, she'd crash.

Life support was at a minimum; some lines had been cut and had bled off both oxygen and other gasses too.

Lights, both interior and exterior, were okay—as most were on sub-systems on an area by area basis.

Food stores were fine. Freezers fine too.

Cargo holds A, B, and D were fine. C had been severely compromised during the Boathi attack and now carried a poisonous atmosphere that was being held with heavy security by the AI systems.

Robo-doc was fine—but he knew that.

Exterior ports all fine except for the lower cargo port, which just kept reporting that it couldn't report to AI. No surprise there since Javor knew that it was jammed. Due to her missing landing gear that had been lost too in the attack, the *Drake* had fallen and that portion had taken the most damage.

"We're not so good," he said.

Sue cocked her head to one side and didn't ask her questions out loud.

"*Drake* will never get back up into space—too many systems are gone. But AI thinks—doesn't know for a fact—that she might fly. But if we take her up—and there's any kind of problem, AI will shut her down and we crash once more. Don't like that at all, as it means that the *Drake* is now just my house on Bones," he said, and his voice was truly perturbed.

Sue nodded lost in thought it looked like to Javor.

Jimmy picked something out of his teeth, and then he looked at Javor.

"So, we're walking to Arlington, I'd guess? If they want us to, that is," he said, referring to the conversation that would have to come next now that the *Drake*'s role had just been finalized.

That sat with them all for a minute or two.

If the *Drake* would never fly again, then yes, if he wanted to find out more about Bones, then he'd have to go to the seat of the planetary government —the Regime who were in Arlington.

Of course, he could simply say the hell with it and as he was now a castaway on Bones, he could live out his years on the planet and stay in the *Drake*.

True though, he thought, *that if the Boathi ever appeared here again, the Drake with its big electrical profile would be found. Which might put me—well, me and Bixby—in jeopardy.*

That's not so good, he thought. *Not so good at all.*

What were the odds that they were even looking for the Drake?

Or perhaps in a few years, with us humans winning the war, the Boathi might be driven from this whole quadrant of space and the Empire would land here instead.

Or ... oh hell, Javor thought, *there was just too much to think on.*

Best to just go one step at a time.

Drake won't fly, so next item is to talk to this Regime group ...

#####

Back at the courthouse after what Javor could claim was the best fried fish he'd ever tasted, the whole Maxwell cadre sat and talked. Cooked this time by Bruce, who said he was the fish guy, there had been large fillets of fish with white flaky flesh, and Javor noted that the others had poured the pink sauce right over top, so he did too.

Delicious.

If nothing else about Bones was good, the few meals he'd had here had been outstanding.

"And this pink sauce stuff is ..." he asked no one special at the table.

Jimmy nodded. "We do have our own small herb garden out back. The pinkness of that sauce comes from something we call the krow plant—pink flowers that if picked at the right time add a kind of lemony hint with a type of anise flavor to anything you pour it on. The fish was simple river trout—we caught them a few weeks back and froze the fillets, but fried up in fat, they are great," he said as he eyed the remaining stack of fillets still in the center of the table.

"Tomorrow for omelets," Sue said, "as I'm on brekkie duty," and that got a big grin from some at the table.

She sat back and looked at him.

"Javor—you seem to be a pretty plugged-in guy when it comes to handling yourself out in the field.

So it would be no surprise for you to learn that
since the *Drake* came down, I've been reporting on
the ship and you—and yes, even on Bixby—to the
Regime in my nightly ham radio reports," she said,
and her tone was a bit apologetic.

But he knew that, of course. Anyone like her and
her cadre would be required to keep the home office
informed, so this wasn't really news.

"You might be surprised to know that we were
told that if you presented problems—if you seemed
like you were going to put Maxwell out of balance
between our cadre and the zombies—that we were
told to terminate you. No questions asked. Balance
is what is important here on Bones, so that too
should not be a surprise. Should it?" she said, and
again her tone, he thought, was one of
appeasement.

He nodded.

*Would have done the same in the Regime's place, and
the Empire too would offer the same advice.*

He smiled and nodded. There was no need to say
more, and Sue leaned in toward him at the table.

"So, last night—before our foray today over to
the *Drake*, we were told that in no case were we to
do anything to you. Keep you up and alive and
happy was the term, I believe. And we don't know
what happened to change that viewpoint—but after
talk among us, we thought you should know before

you speak to the Regime," she said.

He did wonder at that—*why she'd offer up this nugget of information that seemed to blow the whistle on her orders was odd. But then, there was no way to learn that here—the answer was with the Regime.*

He nodded and Bixby, who'd apparently just come over for some affection, licked the hand that sat on his left hip.

He rubbed the dog's ears and welcomed the break in the conversation, but he realized that he'd just learned a fact that might one day be important, if he could learn what happened in the Regime yesterday to change his status.

"Fine, Sue ... and thanks for that background," he said quietly, still rubbing Bixby down, and he picked up one paw to look at the dog's nails. Recently clipped—dew claws removed. He looked inside Bixby's closest ear, and he saw it too was clean. He lifted the edge of Bixby's top lip and noted too that the teeth were fully mature, unstained, and had no tartar.

"Your dog appears to have been pretty well taken care of," Bruce drawled, "so that would explain what we found in his owner's bag ... least we think it was the owner 'cause there was dog food in same."

Javor had forgotten all about that but turned with a start to Bruce.

"Which is—" and he waited.

Bruce looked at Sue, who nodded, and he then got up to go down the mezzanine-wide hallway to a door that sat down the hallway a bi. He went in and came right back out a moment later, carrying that shoulder bag.

He put it on the table after Jimmy had cleared away some of the dinner dishes, and once there was room, he spilled the contents on the top of the table.

Two folded robes that looked old but had been well taken care of.

What looked like a towel was next, and as Bruce unrolled it, a pair of knives—throwing knives—clattered on the tabletop.

Three books. One looked like a journal or log or diary that looked well used. The second book was on first aid, and surprisingly, the third back was on the pack theory of dogs.

A small bag of dog kibble too.

Some kind of energy or food bars too, more than a dozen, and Bixby smelled them and sat up straighter, but nobody gave him one.

Ammo—nine millimeter, it looked like—in pistol magazines that held twelve rounds each.

Big handle on that gun, Javor thought, *as his Colt mag held only nine shells.*

And an electronic tablet. When touched by Bruce, the screen lit up, so it had power too.

But Javor noted it was also a secure screen that needed a password, a PIN, or thumbprint to gain access, and Bruce agreed and said, "Nope, couldn't get in either."

The next item was a loose stack of papers with some kind of clip holding them together, all typed in neat galactic English.

Javor pointed and Sue nodded.

"Yeah, we've read them all. Paperwork is signed by someone called Adamson—directing this guy to take his K9 to Maxwell to investigate the uprising. First, we know of no such person, nor of any uprising either. All a mystery, but the K9 refers, we think, to the dog—your Bixby. This guy was on some kind of a mission, in someone's forces—but none that we know of around here," she said.

"And you did send word back to the Regime on these items too, did you not?" Javor inquired, and everyone nodded.

He sat for a moment.

That Bixby had been trained by someone to be a K9 dog was no surprise.

He knew his stuff for sure, and Javor was glad for that.

He'd been accepted as the new master too.

But this uprising? And a lieutenant in which man's army would be just as important to learn too.

He shrugged. "Time maybe for that call to the

Regime?" he asked.

Everyone stood and they went down the mezzanine-wide hallway to the door that Bruce had left open.

Inside, there was a long table against the far wall with what looked like electronic receivers, amplifiers, and monitors. At the center, there were some tabletop microphones sitting, and above those on a white board was a calendar with notations for almost every single day.

"We change the frequency daily, to prevent any eavesdroppers; we change the filters too, and the new ones get transferred to us at the end of each month for the coming one," Sue said as she dropped into the center chair and patted the one beside her on her left for Javor to take.

He took the chair and noted that she read and then re-read the settings on the calendar before plugging those new numbers into the big black-faced receiver in front of her, again checking twice. Filters were done the same way, and she clicked three times in rapid order with the button on the side of the tabletop microphone in front of her.

As she did so, the receiver beeped at her, and she made one more adjustment. There were three answering clicks on the small set of speakers at either end of the equipment lineup, and she spoke as she depressed her mic button.

"Cadre nineteen, calling. Cadre nineteen," she said and then let the button go.

Moments later, a voice came back to them over those speakers.

"Hey there, Sue ... how's the big town of Maxwell doing today?" The voice was almost playful and sounded young, which was a nice surprise to Javor as he figured the Regime would be full of old guys like him.

"Fine, Trevor, just fine. I've got the space pilot sitting right here beside me and wanted to talk—if we can—but it was all arranged with Vera, can do?" she asked, and that got a positive reply from Trevor.

"And"—there was a click or two—"Vera is on the air, signing off," Trevor said as control of the call went to Vera.

Sue smiled. "Vera, good to speak to you again. I have Javor here with me—he's the fellow who came down on the ship a few days back, and yes, we have news on same—but I'd like to let him tell you," she said.

There was silence at the other end for a bit and then a simple "Go ahead, Javor."

He took the mic, and pressing the send button, he told his tale of being ambushed by the Boathi twenty lights away and of their flight to Bones, all hands dead except himself being tucked into the robo-doc. He told of finding Maxwell and his last few days learning about Bones, and he was careful to include that Sue and the local cadre had been very helpful. And lastly, he shared about the trip back to the *Drake* just hours ago and the bad news about her future. She'd be a great house on Bones, but she'd never fly again.

He tried to make that sound like a positive thing. That being on Bones was not a sentence of life without hope.

About the Boathi, he did point out, as he was sure that Sue had already done so, that he had no idea if the enemy could track the *Drake* to Bones, nor for that matter if they did find the ship that they could do more than simply blow it up. That was something he didn't want to even think of—but he had to point that out at least.

He pointed out that the *Drake* was an explorer ship and had a huge database of Gallipedia content that was at least eight years newer than whatever Bones had. He shared that the AI on the Drake was leading edge too, which was a real bonus for whomever controlled her at least.

And finally, he spoke about himself, providing his age as well as a bio of a few sentences.

He told Vera that he thought as he was a castaway, he could be happy here on Bones.

Silence from the other end.

The woman named Vera was considering all of this, and after a full two minutes, she finally spoke.

"I'd, or rather we'd, like to meet with you, Javor. More to learn, I suspect, and we'd like that to be done in person. You, however, are two hundred miles away. Which is a problem—not so much the distance, but the time it'd take for us to mount a complete foray through the Badlands to the power station at the Adair Dam and then via the old interstate to Maxwell. We feel—and I'm sure that Sue would agree that if it's speed—that a small group could cut corners and evade the kind of response a huge party like our own would receive.

"Sue, I'm going to talk to those here about this more fully—but what I think we'd want you to do would be to button up the cadre house. All five of you would then take on the job of getting Javor to Arlington, soonest. You'd need to avoid as much as you can, time line-wise," she said.

Sue nodded and leaned on her speak button. "So, I'd hear back, say, tomorrow—when do you think you'd like us to depart?" she asked.

"Tomorrow at the latest," Vera said.

Sue nodded and then she looked sideways at Javor and her lips pursed. "Vera—as the AI on the ship is leading edge. One thought is that should we not all get to Arlington—and yes, I mean Javor— should we not at least have some kind of access to the ship put on hold? Just as sort of an insurance policy sort of," she said.

As he leaned forward to speak at once, she held him back.

Vera thought about that for a moment and then it was almost as if you could see her head nodding at the other mic.

"Good idea. Have him input the controls and overrides into the cadre AI at the courthouse, to be used only after, say, in four months. Access to cadre team only, and if he's not back in those 120 days, we will get access to the *Drake*. If he is back, he can kill the order on our own AI himself. Work for you, Javor?" she asked.

He nodded. Four months would be more than enough time to get to Arlington and back, and yes, it was insurance too.

He said, "Done," and that was that as Sue signed off and the link to the Regime was ended.

CHAPTER FOUR

Taking the same route back to the *Drake* to get supplies for the trip to Arlington was an easy task, unless, of course ,one counted on the zombies that somehow were now standing on the bridge that separated the ridgeline and the *Drake* from the town.

Bruce said it first.

"We can just kill a few, which'd get them to feed, and slip by when they're otherwise engaged," he said.

"Except," Sue said, "the dang bridge isn't wide enough. We've gotta lure them back onto the town side, and then you can pick off a few."

Everyone nodded. Javor left this part of the tactics to the cadre as he learned how to handle larger crowds of the dumb brand of zombies.

Jimmy nodded and taking off his backpack and leaving it and his rifle with Rick, he quickly marched up the street toward the bridge that lay on the left-hand side. He was quiet at first, but as he drew even with the twenty or so zombies who were milling about on the bridge, he began to sing and clap his hands loudly.

"She loved me and I loved her back ... again and again and again," he bellowed out over and over, in what shouldn't have been called a tune.

The zombies paid attention immediately, and the murmurs and soft screechings they made followed them as they began to move off the bridge toward Jimmy. He paused to let them get a bit closer and then went up the street straight ahead to draw them away from the bridge, which was emptying fast.

Sue nodded and the rest hustled up to the bridge, turned to their left to go about halfway across, and then stopped. Bruce jumped up on one of the abutments and carefully took aim at the lead zombies who were trudging after Jimmy.

Bang. Bang. Bang. Bang!

Four shots rang out and four zombies fell as their heads exploded into bloody clouds.

Around them, other zombies noticed, and they slowed their chasing of Jimmy to fall on the new meat that now lay at their feet. The feeding frenzy began as they clambered over one another to get to their downed compatriots.

Jimmy nonchalantly moved away from the mass of same in the middle of the road, took a close path along the building fronts on the one side of the street, and quietly moved back toward the bridge. Not a zombie paid any attention and soon he stood beside them once more, donning his backpack.

Picking up his rifle he said, "Four?"

Bruce nodded. "Four today—wanted to finish off that old ammo."

Sue waved an arm and said, "Let's get going, lads," and she and the group walked across the bridge stepping over the now stripped carcass of some kind of a small animal. Bixby stopped to smell the body but didn't go very close, Javor noted.

They turned left once more toward the *Drake* sitting above them on the ridge line.

"Why were those ones just standing around the bridge," Javor asked.

"They don't eat—well, as far as I know, that kind of animal—a coon I think it's called. But the smell of its blood must have attracted them, and once they got on the bridge, there was nothing to eat— but the smell must have kept them there," Sue said and that got nods from the rest of the cadre group.

"So what did eat that coon?" Javor asked, but nobody knew and they all shook their heads.

At the *Drake*, once again, Javor controlled the AI

to open the front airlock and drop the ladder and the lift, and he and the rest went up same to enter the *Drake*.

Javor noted that the final diagnostics report had come in, and it was no different from the smaller pieces he'd looked at yesterday. The *Drake* would never get out into space again. And flying her in the atmosphere was a risky—very risky—one-time thing as she could come down in an instant.

He thought for a moment about the upcoming hike of more than two hundred miles through all sorts of country, and he went back to his bunk area to find clothes and more importantly, some kind of hiking boots. He had none, but he knew that the Empire marines were issued with same, so he searched under Fawcett's bunk for a pair. They shared the same boot size. He found the boots, which were brand new, with high-top clasps and a tread that'd never wear out. He grinned as he also found two pairs of military-grade compression socks stuffed into them too, and he quickly changed his footwear.

Back on the bridge, he looked for a moment at the group of the five cadre members and their firepower.

"Come with me," he said, and he led the way back to the crew area where he faced an unmarked door.

He asked AI to open the door and had to provide his birth date, just like always, to get it to open.

"Six, thirteen, twenty-two forty-nine," he said, and the pocket door slid open to the *Drake*'s armory.

"You are armed, but the *Drake*, I'd think, has better firepower. If you want to trade up, just take what you think you can handle," he said and moved aside so they could all cram in.

The cadre looked at the rifles, carbines, and shotguns on the far wall, the handguns on the left and right, and the bows and arrows on the third wall.

"No need to look there," Bruce said as he pointed at the bows and moved toward the rifles. There were a couple of long-barreled sniper rifles, which he was quick to take down. He unassembled each and then re-assembled them. He hefted one and then the other, and he snapped the magazines out to check on its load and number of shells.

He smiled. "I'd like to shoot this one," he said as he hefted one he'd liked, and Javor nodded and pointed up front to the airlock doorway.

Sue found nothing as she said she knew her own and would stay with that. Jimmy liked the combat shotgun that Javor also favored, so he took that one. Rick and Wayne chose to stick with their weapons. Javor understood that entirely, knowing that the trust between a shooter and his weapon happened over thousands of rounds in all kinds of conditions. Only sometimes would a new choice come along, he knew.

Up front, Bruce had taken the ladder down to the pile of undergrowth below the *Drake* and had taken a stance standing beside a tree, using the sapling as a prop for his elbow. He squeezed off three shots, then made a change to the sights, and then took three more shots. Javor looked at the target that he must be aiming at. Across the river and down the side street was a big clock that jutted out from the building front over the sidewalk. The first three had hit as the sound of the breaking porcelain sign could be heard all the way back here, but the second three were aimed much better as the sign now hung from its bottom stanchions only. Bruce had cut the top one with his last salvo. That was more than two hundred yards away, Javor noted, which got Bruce a big check box from him. This guy could shoot!

He smiled back up at Javor. "Nice gun—I'll take it," he said.

Back on the *Drake*, Javor sat in the co-pilot's seat, instructing the AI to recognize anyone else who had the security code he was now giving it, and he asked for 128-degree encryption on same. *Best of the best*, he knew.

If someone had this code phrase and its subsequent answering phrase, then the AI was to treat that person as crew—with all authority and verifications intact. So part one of the AI insurance plan was in effect. Only part left was to now insert those two phrases into the cadre AI back at the Maxwell courthouse with the time-delay sub-routine.

He nodded.

All done.

He looked over at the five members of the cadre who were waiting to leave and smiled.

"Been my home, the *Drake*, for over a year almost. Will miss her," he said as he checked his big backpack he'd dug out of storage and ensured he had all the items he'd need.

Ammo, check. Jerky bars, check. Extra socks and clothes, check. First aid kit, check. A couple of drone balls, check, with extra batteries too, Sleeping roll, check. And a host of other little items too like a pack of gum, a waterproof set of markers and paper, and a quick-fire starter too.

Dunno what I'll need, so a bit of most of these should do, he thought and smiled at the cadre members.

"Right—let's go," he said.

Javor and the group went out the front airlock door as he took the lift down with Bixby. At the bottom, he carefully instructed the *Drake* AI to close her up—and that he'd see her in a couple of months. He also made sure that the reactor—the real power of the *Drake* that drove their engines and FTL —was closed down. The fuel rods were slowly retracted from the core by the AI, and Javor watched the display as the eight rods were all stored in their own heavy water baths and the core shut down. He saw the solid orange bars across the display noting that the *Drake* was now on full battery power—and at this level of power requirements, the batteries would last at least nine months.

He grunted and said, "Thanks, AI." The AI didn't understand such comment, but they'd be recorded and archived for whoever might come next.

He smiled one more time as he looked up at her.

Damaged sure, but still the explorer ship, my ship— the Drake ...

Back at the cadre headquarters, Sue was buttoning up the contents of their important documents and papers and the like. As she tucked the last stack into the big folder, Jimmy was hoisting up the final receiver and amplifier that had been all hooked up for their ham radio station.

Javor followed them both, carrying the three table mics and a huge coil of network cabling too, as they went out of the room up on the mezzanine that they used as their administration center and down the hall to the larger rear area room. They walked across the tiled floor, went around and behind the large reception counter to a wide-open vault door, and entered the vault.

"The vault had been used," Sue said, "for the courthouse to store items in—and that's exactly what the cadre does too." All of their secure items were now stored in some of the shelves inside the big steel box, and as she closed the huge door, she spun the wheel at the same time.

"Combination is the day the bombs fell for us here on Bones—four, twenty-five, ninety-three—and it's always right, left, then back to right too. Figured as you've left your own AI insurance to the Drake, we can do the same. No telling who's gonna make it back to Maxwell—this is one hell of a hike," she said and smiled.

She was right, Javor knew, but then surely six of them, heavily armed, capable, and knowing the land and infrastructure could make it with minimal hardship. Surely, he thought, and we have Bixby too. Better ears and a sense of smell too that could work for them.

He nodded and smiled back, and then they all went down the main stairs in the foyer.

Sue and Jimmy both did some kind of manual entry of data to the courthouse AI, and then they both looked at him.

"Passwords—good only in 120 days, mind you— please?" Sue said.

He nodded and half-smiled. "First one is my

birth date, which, for those of you who are mathematically challenged, was fifty-two years ago. It's six, thirteen, twenty-two forty-nine. That one needs to be entered first, correct?" he asked.

Sue nodded back to affirm that.

"And the second one is the color of my first-ever flyer that I got on my sixteenth birthday—and the color was orange. That's the challenge question, right?" he asked, as Jimmy typed in both the query and the correct reply, and then he nodded to Sue.

"Right. Birth date to open up the access gate— followed by the query from AI about the color of your first flyer. If not followed by the word orange, then the access port shuts down. Three tries in five minutes is all that's allowed, too ... to prevent the brute force type of attack. We're good," she said as the courthouse AI chimed three times and the lights on same went to green with a couple set to amber too.

She looked around and shuffled her backpack up and onto her shoulders, once again shuffling it to get a good weight balance.

"Jimmy, Bruce, Rick, and Wayne. Anything else? Have we forgotten anything?" she asked.

"Just that there was supposed to be fresh fish again tomorrow evening," Jimmy said wistfully, and that got a chuckle from her.

"And yes, it's rations for the next month and

some. But we know that the food in Arlington is better than what we get here, now don't we," she said, and that got some nods too.

"Let's get a move on," she said. "Would like to get at least ten miles done today."

As they all turned to walk out of the foyer, the sun appeared and the pink light of dawn lit the grounds ahead. Sue turned back to yell at the AI with her administrator password code, and AI closed the doors behind them. A solid locking mechanism could be heard too.

The courthouse was buttoned up pretty well, Javor thought, *at least from scavengers and the dumb zombie types. Someone with smarts could still gain access, but the AI and its ability to enforce security from the foyer and lobby of the building could not be avoided. A sign reading enter at your own risk could have been left out front, he thought and then shrugged that away. Better to let someone enter and then get AI on its case.*

He noted that Bixby was close to him as if he could tell that this was somehow a different day, and he smiled and ruffled the dog's neck.

He smiled a bit at Wayne who had coupled up with him to follow Sue who took point, and they walked down the courthouse walkway, through the hedge opening, and left toward the river.

Four blocks later, they hit the main street in Maxwell that ran parallel to the river but a few blocks west. Many cars, trucks, and even a streetcar partially filled the street, all with the same fire-blackened exteriors.

"Okay, split up—I'll keep Wayne and Javor—you guys take the far side," she said and Rick, Bruce, and Jimmy trotted across the empty intersection to walk down the far side of the street's sidewalk.

"We do this when there's ambush areas that we've not yet checked out," Sue said as she led the way down the sidewalk in front of them. She again took point, while Wayne dropped back behind him, leaving him in the second spot.

"That way, only half of you could get attacked, leaving the other half to come to their aid, correct?" Javor asked.

Sue nodded, which he also took to mean shut up and so he did.

They moved steadily down the street. Every so often, he glanced across to see the others making about the same time too.

In front of a small neighborhood bodega, a huge pile of grocery baskets that someone had stacked neatly at one time had now fallen over, and the three of them had to climb up and over, making a lot of noise as the plastic broke beneath their feet. He was a bit worried about all that noise, but nothing jumped out at them from the cars out in the street, so they continued on.

At the first cross street ahead, the number of cars still in the street ahead lessened drastically. Sue whistled and the other three joined them. Bixby, who had preceded his group all along, dropped back for a moment and then bounded out into the street as a rabbit or something like a rabbit bolted from a pile of rubble in the gutter.

A sharp whistle stopped the dog in mid-chase, and he returned, went around Javor, and then matched his pace.

Good to know too, Javor thought, *that a simple whistle would bring him back even if he was chasing food. Food,* he thought and then reached up into his top left wide pocket on his vest, and taking a jerky bar out, he peeled off the wrapper and handed the bar to Bixby who was all eyes at this point.

It took him a minute to chew it up, and he caught up with the whole group who now had taken back the middle of the street to move along. Bixby pranced ahead too on occasion to investigate a single car or a pile of rubbish at the gutter.

"Dog helps a bit," Sue said and Javor nodded back. *Did help a lot.*

As the group moved street by street, sometimes on the sidewalks and sometimes right down the middle, they made good time, but it wasn't as quick as Javor had thought it would be.

As the street curled slowly to the east ahead of them, the river could now be seen with a lone bridge across it in the near distance. Not a car, truck, or wreck of any kind was on the bridge, and as they reached the edge of the bridge, Sue stopped them.

"Okay, this is the Coombs Bridge, final one across the river here in Maxwell. We go across her, take the eastern side of the far street, and then in a few miles, get on the interstate to the power station at the Adair Dam. Last time in Maxwell is now, I'd say," she offered and waved back over their shoulders.

Javor took a quick glance backward but not at Maxwell per se. He tried to see if he could find the *Drake* on the far shore up on the ridge line, but it was too far away, he figured.

So he waved. See you soon, he thought.

And like the rest of the group, he walked across the bridge, out of Maxwell, and toward the interstate, whatever it was …

#####

Bixby noticed something, sat down well ahead of the group, and howled.

Something, Javor knew, *had been different enough for him to notice and then set off his howling.*

Long howls, he noted too, *as if he was trying to let*

the whole county know something was up from where he sat.

They caught up to him at the top of the roadway as it dipped down toward a valley, which extended a few miles ahead of them and was at least a mile or two wide. Javor could only guess Bixby had been concerned because the valley was out of sight below them. Enormous concrete ramps stretched out hundreds of yards ahead of them, slowly curving onto the fully elevated interstate highway.

Javor put a hand on Bixby's head and said, "Thanks boy, good dog," and Bixby quieted immediately.

What had been a well-maintained highway long, long ago now stretched out across the whole valley like a suspended line of concrete and steel littered with the remains of cars and trucks. It was old and what would be called wrecked in anyone's language. Yet with its size and breadth as well as miles of it stretching off into the distance, it was an impressive part of the old Ceti4 infrastructure. Not so much about Bones, Javor thought, but then time did play havoc on many things.

Supporting those wide concrete lanes were massive concrete pylons, mostly now covered with ivy or undergrowth that crawled up the hundred feet or so. There was one every three or four hundred feet, each one old and tired. He wondered how long they'd hold up the spans that went from one to another as far as he could see. At the foot of those pylons, the weeds, shrubbery, and undergrowth was so thick you almost couldn't see the bottoms of them.

The on-ramps and off-ramps that had allowed the traffic to get on and off the highway still remained. They slowly rose the hundred feet or so in a slow curved path. Some, like the one ahead a bit, had a few cars on it, while others had none. A few ahead too had what looked like some kind of encampment—most likely abandoned long ago. Javor looked for smoke, which would indicate fire, something that would be needed by anyone who was living in that kind of campsite.

He looked both north and south, up and down the valley, and saw only train tracks—two sets with a spur line far to the east. In between the shining rails, he saw grass, weeds, and overgrowth—things that would never happen if there was any kind of rail traffic. Well east of that spur, he saw some cars that lay like they'd derailed perhaps, but it was too far away, and he didn't bother digging out his binoculars to check.

"The valley itself is mostly farmland, well, it once was. The interstate, as you can see, starts here just outside of Maxwell and goes all the way to the power station at the Adair Dam about seventy-five miles if we can believe the signs," Sue said as she pointed to one of the official highway signs. It was leaning to one side and had been fired upon with what looked like shotgun blasts, but it still read that the Adair Dam was seventy-five miles away.

Jimmy nodded and then pointed at the on-ramp below them a few hundred yards away.

"So, do we take the interstate 'til we can't anymore, or do we stay on the ground?" he asked and that got Javor thinking.

If they took the interstate and ran into trouble—zombies or the like—then there was no way around those troubles. If they took the land route, then there could always be a way around troubles ahead.

"Depends," Sue said, "if we need to make time, then we take the interstate, else we walk underneath," she said. and that got nods all around.

Javor also knew that this was most likely the best thing for them—the balance of safety versus speed of travel.

The six of them all got in a one-two-two-one formation; Sue was on point, Javor and Wayne next, Jimmy and Rick next, and on the tail end was Bruce. He hefted the new gun he carried and said, "Could probably take down a zombie a mile down the interstate with this." While that was most likely a stretch, he still exuded confidence.

Sue led and after a while, she pushed out from

being directly under the long concrete spans above them to run parallel about a hundred feet away. For a reason that nobody knew, the undergrowth directly under those spans was thicker.

Jimmy had the best guess and said, "Most likely, the run-off of rainwater comes right down below via some kind of ductwork, so it'd get better irrigation below the spans ... or maybe not."

At least, Javor thought, *that did make sense, and he grinned when he realized there was no one to ask.*

Bixby really had the lead, as it was his senses once again that made him return to Javor's side and growl.

At his feet, Javor looked down and saw some kind of tracks—fresh tracks—in the small muddy part of the trail they'd been following. The tracks were of a four-legged animal of some kind and larger than Bixby's tracks. Not good, Javor thought as he looked at his dog.

Bixby walked stiff-legged, and that meant something was up. Or coming. Or lying in wait, Javor noted for Sue, and she called a halt just ahead of a thicket of shrubs ahead that was deep and blocked their way.

Sue pointed as she said, "Thicket ahead is like two hundred yards wide, so it's either all the way to the top of that rise to the right or through."

She looked at each of them, and there was not a word said, as one by one they all pointed up the rise to the right. Deflecting a threat, even a perceived threat, just from what might be great cover for an ambush was always a good idea.

"Course," Javor said, "we do have a time line—and every single one of these small off-track safety jaunts costs us time. But yeah, let's go right," he said.

He wanted to argue that firepower was on their side along with real live brains instead of dumb zombie brains, but this was the first morning of the first day. To the right it was, and he, like the rest of them, fell in behind Sue as she took to the right, and they slowly climbed up the rise.

It wasn't heavily covered with weeds and undergrowth, but still, it was tougher getting to the top than any of them had anticipated. Bixby was already up there, at the top of the rise, still doing his stiff-legged walk, but the growl was gone. As they all reached the top and stood half-hidden among the tall sumacs that lay around them, they looked back toward that thicket and Jimmy whistled.

Buried inside that thicket, near the left side, was what looked like a small camp. There were a few containers that had been turned into what looked like some kind of home—there were a few women in front of the camp, doing what looked like laundry duty, while two kids were playing. Laundry hung on some lines off to one side and a couple of caches of food items were bound and hung in cages well above the ground.

He looked at Sue. "Basic encampment, shelter, laundry, women, and kids. But note, not a single man. Wonder where they are," he said and noted Bixby still was acting like there was imminent danger. Not enough to howl or growl at—but still close. Bixby was becoming a great asset, as long as you could read his cues.

"Bixby is still worried, though," he added, and everyone else looked at the dog walking stiff-legged ahead a bit and turned every few steps to look back at Javor.

"Noted," Sue said and looked forward once more into the valley.

Ahead lay a long downhill slope toward the next massive concrete support pylon for the interstate off to their left. The pylon's base was also buried in that same thicket as the encampment, which was not something to worry about, and farther—

"Shh … down," Bruce said as he dropped down into a deep crouch and his new gun came up to rest on his shoulder.

They all dropped quickly, and Javor noted Bixby mimicked them as well.

Off to their right, farther away from the interstate and the encampment, a file of what looked like about twenty people were coming toward the rise but veering off to their own right. *That way*, Javor could see, *they'd avoid him and his group and yet still get around to the other side of the rise.*

Jimmy whispered, "Do you think that they're from the encampment?"

The leader of the file was a woman. She had a bow strung on her back and carried a pack that looked pretty heavy. From what Javor could see, they were all women. Each was armed with bows and quivers of arrows. And each looked like they were loaded down with heavy items in their backpacks, and some carried shoulder bags that were also jammed with something.

As they all went by, Jimmy said, "And where are the men?" Again, his question went unanswered.

The troop below, while only fifty feet away, walked carefully and quietly. All walked in file, following the woman in front of her, without a misstep or even a slip on the loose rocky soil along the side of the rise.

Bixby was under his hand, and he clutched the dog's fur tightly as the dog tried to rise. He leaned right over the dog's ears and said as quietly as possible, "Shh ... quiet, boy ... shh," and the dog complied. Don't know why, but it worked this time. Javor was glad about that as the last of the women went by, and they then slowly dipped down toward the thicket ahead of them.

They continued to crouch and watch, and in twenty more minutes, the line of women entered that encampment. They were greeted with shouts and what looked like a real welcome. They all moved their packs and extra bags into a large pile, and a few of them reached inside those packs to pull out what looked like containers of food and the like.

Kids yelled and some of the women, who'd not gone on the scavenging trip, whooped it up.

Jimmy said, "They were just looking for food, and looks like they found some. Those all look like real old-time packages too ... wonder where the hell they found them?"

Food like what they could see down in that camp hadn't been processed, produced, and put into packaging like that in more than eight years. So where did these items come from? While they couldn't really see what kind of food it was, it obviously was dry goods and the like. Foods that perhaps might last eight years but not without some kind of special preservation like freezing. But freezers took power. And there was no power here in the valley—at least as far as any of them could see.

While they pondered that, a couple of things below happened, and one especially worried Javor.

One of the women from the group who had

passed them whistled. From the container near her, an animal came out, and that was surprising. While it was true that eight years ago, the zoos on Ceti4 had been opened up and the animals set free, Javor had been told most had died. Most were used to getting their food in a bucket at dawn or dusk. Most didn't know how to hunt or forage for food. Most ate each other, and almost all of the larger Ceti4 carnivores died.

Below was animal that Javor didn't know, but a simple look at Jimmy got him an answer.

"Called a Taxa—cat sorta like, eats meat, kills its own food too. Run about fifty pounds like that one too," he said as he tried to relate the information in as few whispered words as could be done.

It had small ears, close to the head, while its muzzle was narrow as was its body. Behind the head was a long dark brown line in the lighter brown fur that ran all the way around the animal. It had the same matching dark fur circling each of its feet as well. Could be the animal that had made those tracks a few hundred yards back, Javor thought.

Javor nodded as he continued to hold Bixby tight.

No sense in getting any kind of trouble started via the animals, he thought.

Sue nodded and then began to crawl farther into

the big clump of sumac, and she was followed by them all, Bixby too. As they went over the top of the rise, which hid them safely, they all rose and strode away as quietly as they could down the rise to the small creek below. There, they followed the creek about a half mile away from the interstate before slowly working their way back toward the concrete pylons that still marched away into the distance.

A couple of miles ahead, they could see a set of ramps, and they were connected with a minor regional road that went down the valley floor in a north-south direction.

Javor fished out a jerky bar and took a chew as he handed the rest to Bixby, who chewed it as he trotted back to the front of their group. Just opening up the package brought Bixby at a trot, and once fed his share, he was back on point, just in front of Sue.

They made good time moving parallel to the interstate, and as they passed over the regional road on-ramp, another sign with shotgun damage appeared.

"Only gone five miles but that's good. Don't have our real working speed yet, and yeah, there'll be blisters tonight. But so far, so good," Sue said.

At the ramp, Sue looked at them and shrugged. "We'd make good time—plus I'd rather sleep up there than down here in the woods. And from what I see across the rest of the valley, ain't a homestead to be seen."

She looked at them, one by one, and when she reached Javor, he nodded too.

Five miles was okay, but judging by the sun and the shadows, not much of the day was left.

It was time to make time ... and the on-ramp to the interstate wasn't even a mile ahead.

At the foot of the on-ramp, Sue had them all stop for a quick rest and to check their weapons and tactical approach too. She went around and looked at all their weapons and made sure that each was fully loaded and on safety but ready to go in an instant.

"Tactically, I'd like Javor to take point with Bixby —that'll give us a real chance at an early head's up should we run into an ambush point, I'd think. I'll take the rear, and you other guys, couple up in the middle," she said.

Taking point was easy—especially with Bixby and his superior senses, Javor thought, and with a nod from Sue, he turned to slowly walk up the center of the two-lane on-ramp that slowly climbed up to the interstate highway in the air.

The road was still in fair shape with a few holes,

pieces of re-bar jutting out, and concrete rubble ahead. The lines that had been painted on the road surface were faded, almost gone in many places, and yet it still was easy to stay about in the middle of the road.

Ahead, Bixby led the way by about twenty yards and often looked back over his shoulder to check on the rest of them. He sometimes ambled from one side of the ramp to the other, smelling and sniffing and cocking his head at a hole or two. Javor thought he must be looking for food and tossed him another jerky bar minus a big bite, and Bixby chomped that up in a few seconds, again trotting ahead of them all. There was only one truck, lying on its side ahead a bit, and as Javor got near, he took a moment to stoop down and look inside the front windshield. All he could make out through the starred broken glass was a burned seat and a skeleton of the driver, dead now for years and devoid of any flesh.

As he straightened up and turned, Bixby suddenly ran off ahead and then turned to the right, onto the merging interstate lanes as they came in from the left to go straight. Javor quickly followed and it took him almost a minute to catch up and access the four-lane interstate that headed east.

Instead of continuing to run ahead after Bixby, he slowed down to look back at the interstate behind them, and he froze in his tracks. There was a fort there.

Behind him, to the west on top of the interstate about a hundred yards back from where the on-ramp joined up, was a set of defensive logs and pointed spears and lances all fixed ahead. Trying to rush that position, Javor knew, would mean impalement, and he was glad to see there were no people so impaled now.

Behind that guardrail-to-guardrail row of fixed spears and lances was a higher row of old pallets once used to ship goods on, which were now vertical and nailed together to form a wall that could be defended. There was a hole in that wall in three spots, but no one stood there. No people, just the fort itself, and Javor looked from side to side. A larger two-story tower had the same pallet walls and an overhang of a cloth cover.

The fort stretched from side to side. There was no way around the thing, unless you could fly, he realized. And not a single pair of eyes that he could see stared back at him.

He turned back to face east and down the interstate ahead, and he saw that Bixby had moved over to sit against the far guardrail, his big tongue hanging out as he panted in the late afternoon sunlight.

Sue was at his side in less than a few seconds as

the other four spread out to take a defensive position around him.

She looked at the fort and then shrugged.

"So, abandoned, right?" she asked.

He nodded. "Or at least empty while the owners are out hunting for their dinners, maybe," he replied and began to walk closer.

He hadn't taken more than a few steps when Bixby bounded right by him. He went right up to a set of spears in the right-hand third, stepped on something they couldn't see, went up and over the spears just behind, and then dove through one of the three open gates in the pallet wall. Moments later, they heard him barking as they broke into a trot to join him.

Up and over the spears was easy as there was a set of three steps. The steps had been built in at such an angle one couldn't even see it from out front. They went through the open doorway into the fort's interior.

Inside were normal items that anyone would have in their living space—a couple of wooden benches and a church pew; a set of dusty mattresses off to one side; three tables with a couple of broken chairs; and a cooking fire pit that had a large hood over it that went straight up and out the roof. Behind all of that were a couple of trucks positioned to form an inner and secure spot to use in case of attack. There were a few bored-out gun ports on each solid metal wall. The side windows were boarded over but had slots carved out so you could still see the enemy. "When there was one, that is," Sue said.

On the north side of the fort's interior was a narrow walkway that went behind the truck, along the guardrail, and then along the open four-lane interstate. From here, they could all see that the interstate only continued for about a few hundred yards. It had been broken up and it stopped a hundred feet from the ground with no way up or down.

"Fort lies in a pretty good location," Jimmy said. "Dead end's over there so nothing can come from behind. Front is protected by the defenses and further ahead are both an on-ramp and off-ramp for access. I'd like to say thanks—'cause this is where we should stay the night, right, Sue?" he asked, but he was already putting down his pack and massaging his shoulder.

She looked around one more time and then nodded. "Sure, we'll camp here. I'll take the first three-hour watch, then Wayne, and then Rick. Bixby will be a big help too, but whoever is on watch, no snoozing!" she said politely, but everyone heard her implied tone behind it.

As they all doffed their packs and set up to make

some kind of dinner, Rick found a cache behind one of the mattresses that was partially leaning on a stack of pallets.

"Hey, bingo, folks!" he said as he dragged out a suitcase—an old, dented, and discolored one, true, but still he forced the lock on same and grinned at them all.

Inside were many cans of soup with red and white labels. Everyone reached in about the same time. Javor was a bit slow, but he got two cans of something called Scotch Broth and he smiled. Lamb and veggies, as he remembered, and then he and the others dug down in the suitcase and found a package of crackers too.

The crackers were still in their original consumer packaging like what you'd find at your local bodega.

There was no discoloration, no dents, and no breaks in the package at all.

He opened up one end, took a bite of a square cracker, and noted that it was still crisp and slightly salted.

"How'n the hell did this last eight years," he wondered out loud.

Nobody answered as everyone was chomping on their own crackers or biscuits.

Bruce lit the fire and got that going, while Rick used a can opener to open up each of the soups. He arranged them on a steel shelf he'd found over in the corner, and with some careful balancing, he got the soup heating up.

In an hour, the soup was gone, Bixby had been fed, and the sound of munching crackers was all that was happening in the fort.

Outside, the sun was setting on the horizon, and the golden and amber light poured in from the slots and holes in the trucks and pallets behind them. Both moons had risen earlier, and now both were on their last quarter portions, shining but not as much as when they were full. Still the light gold tones added to the scenery. Dusk on Bones was always pretty, Javor had noted, and tonight was no different. He leaned against the guardrail and glanced over and down the hundred or so feet to the ground below.

Bathed in that same golden light, the overgrowth and underbrush looked like an award-winning gardener's best work, and he realized he was happy on Bones—at least so far. He ran his hand along the round polished guardrail and noted that except for a stanchion every twenty yards, the round pipe stretched out back to the on-ramp area and then ahead for hundreds and hundreds of yards. And in the dusky sunlight, it looked like it was made of gold, sparkling and glistening into the distance for miles ahead.

He wandered back into the fort interior. After what was probably only an eight-mile hike, most of the group was tired and had already taken a mattress and begun to get ready for sleep.

Sue got up and stretched. "Looked up at that tower earlier, and yes, she'll do. I'll take early watch as of now and will come and wake up Wayne in three hours. After his three-hour watch, he'll wake up Rick, and we get up when Rick's time is done. Should be just after dawn by then, so night, all—but do keep your guns close by, eh?" she reminded them, got her own rifle, and went over to the left to climb the stairs up to the tower.

Javor noted that one of the mattresses was not claimed, so he dragged it over to the far right side behind the pallet wall. He put his sleeping bag on top, took his boots off, and then climbed in the sleeping bag.

His shotgun he lay on the floor, just beside the edge of his mattress, and he whistled quietly for Bixby, who came over from out front and climbed over him to lie on the unused part of the mattress. He curled up and was snoring inside five minutes. Javor shook his head. A dog's life was something to have.

He slowly drifted off, one arm under his head and the other on top of his shotgun, and the dreams came once again.

He was racing in the decathlon once more, but this time, he was still chasing the leader in the fifteen-hundred-meter dash, and he was behind by about three steps.

Behind but gaining.

Inch by inch, he pushed his toes even farther into the tips of his spikes, asking for the most spring he could from his thighs.

Yard by yard, he gained until he was even … until the race could be his.

His thighs were screaming at him while the balls of his feet were being rubbed raw inside his spikes as he stretched and reached down for every single ounce of effort.

Something changed, and the hail now worried him. The sound of large balls of hail hitting the track and the world around him was suddenly in his consciousness, which was so odd, so different.

Almost before Bixby began barking, he was up and kneeling with his gun in hand.

It wasn't hail at all.

The sound of rifle fire and dozens of arrows banging into the pallet wall in front of him that had woken him. He heard Sue's rifle up top begin to bark as she fired back.

He rolled to his left, took up an edge position in the right-hand doorway of the front pallet wall, and took a quick peer out at the starlit night and the interstate ahead of him.

Shots rang back at them, and Jimmy and Bruce found slot holes to accept their rifle muzzles and fired back too. Rick was up in the tower and firing. He couldn't see Wayne, but he heard moaning from behind him, but that would need to wait until the threat was over.

From his vantage point, he could see only shapes, but shapes of people who obviously wanted them dead, so he hefted the shotgun, threw off the safety, and emptied three shells into whomever was out there.

CHAPTER FIVE

As the *Sophon* came out of FTL and slowly
moved toward low orbit over the planet, the sub-
alternate was anxious as his captain stood for no
mistakes. He guided the raider ship gently—no
sudden pushes of acceleration or nudges—as the
ship slowly rotated to sit with the bridge looking up
at the planet.

The view, if he'd been allowed to comment about
it, was spectacular as this was a system with two
stars—a G-class yellow star and a small red dwarf
star, and the light from the two of them bathed the
world above with glows of red and yellow making
the shadows a dark orange. Under such lighting,
the seas and oceans looked like dark masses of
swirling red and orange waters. The continents too
had an odd coloration as well. In the northern

latitudes, the snow and ice around the polar cap looked bright red in color, while the more temperate landmasses were the traditional browns and yellows.

He shrugged and sped up the ship to get around and below the terminator, the line where the lack of sunlight made it nighttime. But here in this system, with the two stars instead of one, the area that was dark was very narrow.

Normally, it would be half a planet wide as the darkness faced away from a single sun. But here, because the two stars were together, the red dwarf rotating, the records showed, around its yellow mate, the darkness was a wedge above them, barely six hours each night.

He nodded and then used the scanners to look for power, for lights, or for any technology that could be seen to indicate that the planet had been rejuvenated from its bombing eight years ago. And there was none.

He checked for nuclear power and got nothing indicating that any kind of fusion or fission was occurring on the planet at all.

He checked for electromagnetic lines and found none; no power was being moved across the planet via lines or networks.

He checked for lights even closer, drilling down onto regional and then specific areas of scanning too and nothing.

He looked at major rivers where they met the oceans, seas, and even large lakes, and he found only desolation and ruins.

And finally, he checked for the *Drake,* the ship they were hunting for, and its FTL and Ansible trail.

No trail at all. He checked, then double-checked, and made the decision that wherever the Drake had gone, it had not come to this planet.

No civilization at all was his summary.

Time to call the captain and report.

He shuddered but still he knew his report was correct...

#####

In the thicket that lay a mile away, the sound of gunshots—many, many gunshots—was awakening the whole camp. Three of the women in one of the smaller tents burst out and were in the process of getting others up at the same time. One woman came out of the container to the far side of the center of the camp, her cat the Taxa at her side, and waved to them all.

"Shots. We know where that's coming from—so let's get going. Remember, take lives and then their arms," she said as she trotted off down a narrow path through the thickest part of the thicket. Behind her, more than two dozen others followed in single file as they made excellent time and cleared the thicket in less than a couple of minutes. They ran now, full tilt, the Taxa leading the way as they took the side of a rise ahead and motored around it toward the on-ramp that was now only a few hundred yards ahead.

The Taxa made even better time, and while the number of gunshots had slowed and almost stopped, the cat stretched out its gait and ate up the rising ramp quickly. At the top, it dived for the edge of the merging lanes from the left and slowed as it hid and crawled along that edge.

The leader of the women did likewise, and all of them now hid behind the edge of the merging lanes, keeping their heads below the guardrail but still tipping up a head to see when they could.

Ahead of them were more than a dozen of the attackers, all with either rifles or bows. Most were dressed in rags—shirts with no arms and jeans with holes and missing legs even.

She knew who they were—zombies that were smart zombies but not so much.

Something had happened to them that made them different from others, and while they were smarter than the normal type, they still didn't understand language. Tools, and yes, weapons they could master, but that was all.

141

She and her tribe had killed every single one they'd ever found—and here were a dozen or so more.

She shook her head. *More to kill.*

One of them—waved a trio over to the guardrails and dipped his hand down suddenly to indicate some kind of move.

"Must have been the leader," the head woman said to herself.

The three zombies crept over slowly toward the far right side of the highway and hid behind a stack of those pallets.

And as she watched, the three attackers went right up to the guardrail and pulled out what looked like some kind of wire harnesses. One served to help the others as each of them thrust an arm deep into what looked like a big curved hook. There were a couple of buckles to fasten, but soon all three of them had their own arms extended by the wire harnesses that ended in that big solid steel hook.

One by one, they hoisted themselves over the edge of the guardrail to then grab ahold of the circular rail itself with that hook. Sort of like a giant fishhook, the woman thought, and while she could no longer see the lead attacker over the edge, she could see that he slowly moved the first hook to his right a few feet and followed that with the hook

142

attached to his left hand next. Slowly he crept away, the hook making no noise at all and the guardrail wall covering his presence. The next man did the same and then the third man too. All were now sliding along the outside of the guardrail, unseen by the people inside the fort. All would be surprised when they were suddenly flanked by them too, she noted.

A gunshot rang out from the fort's tower, but she heard the ricochet as that bullet missed its target.

"It's time," she said to herself and slowly brought up the woman behind her so that they were now two deep behind the wall of the merging lanes. She held out a fist and then two fingers, and they all strung an arrow and waited.

She rose just enough to see that ahead of them were only ten attackers. Up on the interstate they were closer to the stars, but still the enemy was hard to see clearly.

Her front row was nine strong, so the second row would finish these zombies off, and then it was just the three over on the guardrail.

She counted down, and at one, she and the front nine rose smoothly, drew their bows, and the arrows flew.

Seven fell in an instant, and as the remaining two began to look around, the front row of women squatted down and the second row rose and loosed their arrows. The remaining twosome died where they stood.

The second row then squatted too.

The lead woman called out to the fort as she got someone to hold her Taxa by the scruff of its neck. "We've just killed your attackers—zombies. Could that earn us a talk?" she said. She rose slowly, leaving her bow on the ground, and walked very slowly around the lead edge of the ramp wall and turned to her left to face the fort.

No shots, which is good.

"However, there still are three of them on the right-hand side over the guardrail who're crawling past you to flank you. You might look at that about now," she offered as she pointed at the area where the attackers would probably be now.

From inside, a single man came out, wearing a jumpsuit, vest armor, and a shotgun, if she knew her arms, on his chest.

Beside him, a dog appeared too—and she was glad that her Taxa was behind her and being held back.

He walked toward her cautiously until he reached the body of the first attacker. He checked that the zombie was dead. He checked them all, which took another minute or so, and she grew nervous.

"Sorry, but those three are about—"

The sound of gunshots—four gunshots—rang out, and from a distance away, she heard "Yippee, got 'em all."

The man in front of her pushed his shotgun down and to his side and came closer.

"You the group from back in that thicket behind us near the last pylon?" he asked.

She nodded.

"You women aren't zombies, right?" he asked.

She nodded.

"You mind telling us why you'd kill off these zombies—they weren't attacking you. We do thank you though," he said, and he dipped his head as a sign of respect.

She nodded. "We know this type of zombie. They can master tools and arms and as well, we now see, some kind of tactical thinking too. They eat us—or any flesh at all, really. So we kill all we find of them, as they would have come down the on-ramp to our own encampment sooner or later. So no thanks needed, really," she said.

From behind him, a woman was helping one of their group, who had taken an arrow in his arm.

She carefully lowered him down onto a pallet that lay in front of them, reached back into her pack, and pulled out something that she clicked— and the area lit up with light. She placed it in one of the group member's hands and then helped the wounded man take off his upper body clothing to get to the wound.

The arrow had pierced the man's left bicep and had gone halfway through the arm. He winced and nodded, and the woman grasped the arrow behind the entrance point with both hands.

"On three, Wayne," she said, and as she counted from one, she broke the arrow in half when she got to two.

"Yeah ... I knew you'd cheat," he said and groaned as she slowly slid the arrow ahead and out of his arm. No spurting blood came out, so the woman said, "Missed the big artery" and then held out her hand.

From the other side, the man with the shotgun handed her a pouch of something, which she carefully sprinkled within the wound on both sides. She accepted a series of bandage materials and slowly bandaged up the wound.

The man with the shotgun turned back to face her, and he looked at her directly, staring into her face as if seeking something.

"And there is no price either, for your help?" he asked, and she had a feeling that he was aiming at something, but she still had to demand her price.

"We'd like to take their arms—all guns and ammo as a price. Would that be okay with you?"

Worried she might add more to her price, he

nodded and said, "Fine by us. Take all of them. We don't need them."

Bixby growled and the man looked at his dog.

"You have a Taxa, yes?" he asked as he looked back and over her shoulder.

She nodded and waved her arm to signal that her group could now stand up and come forward. One of them held a tight grip on the Taxa's collar to prevent any kind of an issue.

The man said, "Down, Bixby," and the dog sank to lie on the concrete highway.

As the rest of the women came up to stand behind their leader, Javor waved too. From behind him, the balance of his group came out of the fort and stood with him as well.

He looked at one of them and tilted his head.

"Yup, Javor—got all three. The last one saw it coming though and just unhooked himself from the guardrail and dropped. Don't think he could fly, so he's as dead as the other ones just hanging there. Nice trick though ... I woulda never thought of that one," Jimmy added.

The woman who'd done the wound dressing stood back up. "My name is Sue. I'm the leader of this group, and we are a Regime cadre. Our headquarters is over in Arlington, which is where we're headed—and I'd like to thank you for your help today too," she said as over the far horizon to the east a pink wash was now appearing. Dawn was coming and as the light was now better, the scruffiness of the dead around them was very much a matter of both smell and distastefulness.

"We wish you luck—the interstate is fraught with peril, and you should always be on guard," she said as she stepped forward. "And my name is Josie, and we call ourselves the Interstate Tribe because of where we live and where we control our destiny."

Javor nodded and was going to ask more but was interrupted by Sue.

"We need to get a move on—we've only got so many days to get to Arlington and back," she said and smiled.

"Maybe when we come back this way in a couple of months, we can drop by your camp and we can chat further. For instance, I'd like to know why the Interstate Tribe has no men and where you got those food items from yesterday—but that can all wait," she said.

Josie was surprised but didn't show it and she nodded. "We would be honored to have you visit when you're back this way—just be cautious at your approach, and that'll work fine," she said. She turned at that point, took her Taxa from another woman who looked glad to give up that handful of collared fury, and then smiled as she turned to her right and picked up her bow.

Josie turned back around. "Remember—travel on the interstate is much quicker, but always be vigilant—at least as far as the Adair Dam. That's as far as we ever go, but be careful—and if you find this sign, it's our own meaning the area is safe," she said as she pointed at the arrow with a star halfway along same, the star spray-painted in green and the arrow in blue.

Javor nodded and again dipped his head as the tribe of women slowly moved to the right to go down the on-ramp and back to the ground.

Sue nodded. "I've got point—well, Bixby does—but then me, and Javor would you take the rear, please" she said as she turned and marched away down the interstate staying to the left as the on-ramp was on the right. Ahead lay miles and miles of concrete …

#####

Walking along in tactical formation on the interstate began to wear on the group, as mile after mile presented nothing but a few cars or trucks, long since holding anything of interest. Burned wreckage was all they found. Bixby continued to be up on point, but Sue had dropped back from point to walk with Wayne and Jimmy, while Rick, Bruce, and Javor followed a few footsteps behind.

"Think we're okay with this," Sue said, "as there's nothing that can get to us without showing up hundreds of yards ahead—or behind us too. Javor, you do need to look back every so often, right?" she asked, and he grunted a yes back to her.

After another hour or so, Sue called a short rest break, and each broke out something to snack on.

Whistling for Bixby, he took a bite of another of the dog's favorites, the jerky bar, and tossed it at him. As Bixby smacked his lips, those big canine teeth shiny and white, the dog looked at him for seconds and got a head-shake instead.

"Not now, boy—later," Javor said, and the group started up again.

Jimmy said, "We're heading like southeast, right?"

Sue nodded.

"So then if one were to look back at the northwest saw that huge line of black on the horizon, what would one begin to think?" he said as he stopped and turned to look behind them.

On the horizon lay a black bank of clouds with gray above. As they watched, the black shelf clouds were coming closer. Even this far away, one could see that they reached from the ground up high and higher still, foreshadowing what could only be called an enormous storm.

"A bloody big storm on its way," Sue spat out,

"and it's looking like it's a nor'wester too."

She went to the edge of the interstate, looked over first, and then back as far as she could..

Then she did the same thing but looked ahead, as far as she could.

She shook her head.

"We've already come almost six miles from the last ramp—and if I look ahead, I don't see any more ramps for more miles than that. So we'll need to find a car or truck to weather this out—let's double-time it to the next group," she said as she hoisted her backpack up a little higher and turned to take the point again.

"Move out," she said, and they all began to trot at a good clip.

Ahead, about a half mile, they could see another group of vehicles, and then as the interstate slowly angled to their left, another group lay ahead. The trot wasn't too bad. Javor slowed for a moment as the boxes of ammo for his Colt tucked way down at the bottom of his backpack had twisted to rub on his spine. He shifted the pack, which moved the ammo off his vertebrae, and he sped back up to catch the group.

As they came closer the first group of vehicles, Sue stopped a hundred yards away and looked back.

"We've got like maybe an hour or so is all—FYI,"

she said as she looked at Javor and held out her hand.

He nodded, said, "Bixby — with me," and slowly walked toward the vehicles.

Someone eight years ago had been following a little too closely to a big truck that carried a flammable liquid cargo — and when the bombs fell, they'd not braked in time and had plowed right into the back of the truck.

That had probably made it ignite and slide sideways on the four-lane interstate, which had made four cars in the middle lane all crash into each other and the truck too. Two of those cars were squashed under the truck, which now lay canted to one side, almost up against the steel guardrail. The other two had run into an RV, which also must have been involved in the accident too.

All of the vehicles had burn stains on them, little glass in the windows and windshields, and two of the cars had also been stripped of the interiors. No seats were left, no headliners, and no door panels ... just plain metal, connecting rods and pins, and carpet that had been half-burned and half-stained with what looked like carrion fodder.

Few skeletons, Javor noted, as he slowly walked up from the back right side. He prodded each of the cars with his shotgun, giving it a smack to see what might come out, and nothing did. No scavengers at least, he thought.

The big liquid cargo truck had been tilted to one side with one car half-buried under its rear wheels. He banged the big steel tank and it rung like a bell —but again nothing crawled out from under it.

He put down his backpack and gun, got on top of one of the rear tires, and used it to climb slowly up the stained outer steel shell of the liquid tank. He reached the top mounted door to the tanker cargo hold in a few careful seconds.

Pulling out the Colt, he looked at the mechanism of the door lock. It was not protected by a security panel or any kind of technology. Only a simple safety, holding down a latch.

Clicking the safety took a bit. He had to turn the Colt on its back and use it like a hammer, but the safety finally swung to OFF. He lifted the latch carefully, pulled back the round manhole cover, and held his breath.

Empty. Leaked out the contents long ago, he thought.

No smell at all, but it did have some light within from below where the tank had been pierced by the two cars. One had ripped a slash in the bottom that was about five feet long but only a few inches wide. The other had buried its hood and the engine into a crease in the tank it'd made, and that hole was a couple of feet across.

He could also see the remains of whatever the cargo might have been staining the very bottom.

But it was empty and again no scavengers. He clicked on the flashlight that was attached to his vest belt, and the tank lit up inside.

It was empty. Someone had been in there though because the remains of a fire were directly below the manhole at the foot of the ladder that connected the top and bottom of the tank. As well, car seats had been dragged in up front too. Someone had camped here for a while, he figured.

He took a couple of steps downward, shined the light to both ends, and then made the conclusion that yes, they could all take refuge here if that storm was going to be the doozy it was supposed to be.

Moving back and up from the inside, he propped the door out of his way, cautiously slid down the curved side of the tank to the wheel frame assembly, and then dropped over the tire to the concrete once more.

Bixby was sitting there, looking at him, one paw on his backpack, as if to say "where you been?" and he smiled at the dog.

Sue, however, was also there, her head cocked to one side.

He nodded to her. "Interior is fine—totally dry and we'd survive any kind of storm," he said as he glanced sideways behind Sue.

The storm was closer, much, much closer, and it was lit up occasionally by lightning. No thunder, he noted, just the flashes of jagged lightning. As he stared, he thought he saw a tornado funnel cloud off to the east.

He nodded once more. "Someone else has been in same, there's a fire pit that was used. Light too, from those two cars that plowed into the truck and pierced the tank, which is, yeah, empty. We'll make out fine, I'd bet," he said.

Sue smiled. "Hope so—'cause it's all we got," she said, as she left the group to walk one time all around the whole pile of vehicles.

She came back in less than a minute and said, "Then it's the truck for us today and tonight—well, until that nor'wester goes on by. I've checked too for the truck—she's a Faraday cage for us. Whoever made this thing ensured that the cargo would not be affected by a lightning strike—the copper wires that carry the current are still there and fine. She's insulated is what I mean, so even though it's the tallest metal structure here on this part of the road, we should be fine. And we're going to be the cargo today, so let's get in, shall we?" She hoisted off her backpack, and they all got to the business of getting to safety.

Bixby, however, proved to be a problem as he would not let Javor nor anyone else help to get him up on top of the truck.

Sue watched the dog whine and twist out of their

grasp and said, "Hey, let me, but first, Javor, you get in the truck and then go forward to that hole by the front car."

He complied with the request quickly. Moments later as he sat in the tank and looked out of the hole, he saw Sue with the scruff of Bixby's neck in her two hands, dragging the dog toward the hole.

"Call him, Javor," she said, and he did that too as he dropped to half-lie over the hole and held out his arms.

Hearing his name, but not seeing Javor, Bixby scrambled up on the side of the car, then inched forward to stand on the buckled hood, and looked up at his master. Whining, the dog got closer and then slowly stepped up onto the crease of the truck tank. Bixby half-jumped, half leapt, into Javor's arms.

Grabbing the dog, he smiled, hoisted him within, and said. "Thanks, Sue, I owe you one."

Everyone got inside and Bruce pulled a large lantern out of his pack. Closing the door above, he hung the lantern on the stairs high enough to provide light for all. Each moved to take up some private space within the tank. Javor noted that Bixby wouldn't move much away from the hole in the bottom of the tank, so he camped out there, lying out on one of those car seats that was close to the hole.

Bruce climbed the ladder, opened up the door, looked out, whistled, and came back down in a hurry.

As he did, the tank began to ring from hail pelting it as the storm front reached the interstate. The hail made the tank ring loud and like a bell. The wind too was something else to reckon with. It began to pound on their ears, as it made little pieces of the vehicles around them fly away, banging into the cars and the truck tank with loud echoes and ricocheting metallic sounds.

"Big front, and yes, I saw lightning too," he added, which was verified by the flash of light that bounced off the concrete below the truck and flashed up inside the holes there.

They got comfortable. Javor dug into his pack, took out Bixby's kibble, fed the dog, and poured out fresh water for him. As Bixby ate, Javor had a couple of his jerky bars and figured that was his late lunch or early dinner for today. Sue had joined him up front on the other car seat, and they both grinned at each other as they ate.

Farther back, Wayne was sitting on a wooden box that had probably been earmarked as firewood but hadn't been used. Rick was farther back, lying right on the tank with his head on his backpack, and was almost snoring in minutes. Bruce sat behind the ladder area, and he'd found a pile of some kind of papers, perhaps again for the fire, but he'd wadded them up and lay on them as the tank was hard to lie on. Jimmy had simply taken the easy way and lay down on the cold metal curved floor of the tank, and he was snoring already.

They all kept pretty still, as the lightning flashes were still silent yet showed up via the holes in the tank. They all sat and waited as the storm grew louder and louder and the winds picked up to what sounded like hurricane speed.

A huge flash of light coming inside meant that a lightning bolt had hit close. The air around them inside the truck tank seemed to ionize and get sharp smelling with ozone. As the winds that followed surged, they heard a piece of one of the cars torn off by the strong winds smash into the truck tank before whirling off the interstate. And the winds grew louder and the lightning lit up the interior of the truck tank more often. The center of the storm was upon them.

Another flash of light hit something close, and the truck tank suddenly lurched to one side, falling a couple of feet off one of those cars it had sat on before, and jammed up now against the guardrail.

When the next large lightning bolt hit the truck directly, it ionized the air a split-second before the bolt hit, and while Javor's brain told him it was going to happen, even so, his whole world went black…

CHAPTER SIX

The truck was dark as the winds howled and the rains were driving down onto the interstate.

The truck had fallen but hadn't rolled as much as it fell and twisted even more so to one side. The manhole cover that was propped up halfway open was suddenly gone too, and while it was black out that hole, one could see the lightning often as it continued to pound the truck tank and the interstate too.

Sue came to first and began to call out names in the dark as the lightning had burned out the lantern.

That woke Javor, and his right knee was flexed up tightly, cramped up against his hamstring. The bolt that had hit them had been the culprit, and his alien tissue had reacted badly. He flexed the knee

160

out straight, slowly, a little more extension each time, until the pain subsided, and he tapped his vest belts to find his flashlight and clicked it on.

Bruce was at the far end, and he waved at them as he slowly groaned and rolled off his paper bed. He looked to his left and said, "Jimmy?" and then he yelled it again as he scrambled to get to the man.

Jimmy had been lying on the bare metal floor of the truck tank, and with those millions of volts coursing through same, he had not survived the bolt. Bruce hovered above him trying to do CPR.

Rick too had been on the metal floor, and Wayne was above him doing compressions by the time that Sue and Javor crawled back to help.

One look at both Jimmy and Rick and they both knew it was a lost cause.

Sue held out a hand to stop them, and they did that begrudgingly.

"They were lying right on the metal tank floor … still, it should have been okay—this truck was built to take direct lightning hits," she said, and the words were like darts as she spit them out.

Jimmy and Rick. Gone.

Javor turned with a start to look for Bixby, and as he aimed his flashlight back toward the front of the truck, the dog sat up on the shard of carpet that it'd been lying on. "He's safe," Javor said to himself. The carpet must have had some kind of backing of rubber.

"We'll have to ride out the rest of the storm, but I'd say we all need to get off the floor of this truck," Sue said, and she went up front to drag her car seat back toward the surviving group members.

Javor nodded, did the same, and ensured that Bixby sat beside him on the car bench seat too.

Bruce and Wayne did likewise and also used the rest of the pile of wood pieces to stay above the floor of the tank.

And the rains now came in full force.

The round manhole entrance to the tank on the roof was like an open pipe of water as it poured in by the gallons to run toward the rear of the tank, and it began to fill up that area. As the tank was now slanted toward the back of the truck, where Javor, Sue, and Bixby were near the now half-sealed hole on the bottom of the tank, it was not a cause for much concern as yet. Bruce and Wayne slowly moved toward the front too and passed the ladder area, ensuring they remained off direct content with the floor.

It was five hours, by Javor's count, *that the storm raged outside.* He massaged his knee as it reacted badly to the change in atmospheric pressure that came with a storm. The alien tissue seemed to have a slow burning sensation, and he rubbed it over and over.

Five hours of sitting here with the bodies.

Five hours of the driving rain and the lightning bolts slowly moving away as the front moved on.

Five hours that they sat wet, sad, and yet somehow still glad to be alive.

He threw Sue a half-smile once, and she returned it with a tilt of her head.

Five hours was a long time to grieve, he thought, *but he hadn't even known the two men long.*

He was snoozing when Bixby licked his forehead, and he slowly came to and saw that the rain had stopped, the winds had died down, and a bit of sunshine could be seen outside.

He looked at Sue and pointed to Bixby and she nodded.

Moving slowly, dragging his gear and shotgun behind him, he slowly shepherded Bixby toward the hole in the front of the truck tank and was pleased to see that it was no longer over the hood of the car. He dropped the dog down the couple of feet to the concrete itself. He dropped down too, and they both moved by going on all fours below the cab of the truck to get back out into the center of the roadway.

He stood and then as Sue and the other two joined him, they stared at the pile of vehicles in front of them.

A lightning bolt had hit one of the cars near the

end of the pileup and had moved it and some of the closer cars over what looked like four feet at least. The big bang that they'd heard, no doubt.

Another bolt had smashed into the bumper area of one of the cars, and the bumper itself had been launched over, embedded into the very front of the truck tank, and wrapped around the guardrail.

Sue looked at that closely. She grabbed it and tried to rock it, and it wouldn't budge. She nodded.

"Our lightning-bolt-proof truck was beaten by this simple bumper. The bolt that hit the bumper moved it to link the truck tank to the guardrail, making the tank not a Faraday cage to protect the cargo—us—but a direct link to the ground. All guardrails are grounded on all highways to protect them—so we were beaten by a bumper—and Jimmy and Rick paid for that dearly," she said.

She shook her head. "We'll leave them there— maybe we'll collect their personal effects, but they'll stay in that tank. As a note to anyone else that the tank is not to be trusted in a nor'wester. Wayne, please go back and get their effects—arms too, please, as we can't have them fall into zombie hands," she said as she quietly leaned on the guardrail.

Ahead of them, the storm still raged, but it was moving along like a clipper, and there were big round clouds and some sunshine occasionally here.

As Javor looked ahead, he could see the next on-ramp as it climbed up to the interstate, and it was only a few miles ahead.

"We'd maybe get off the highway say at the next ramp and make camp down on the ground—that sound okay?" he asked.

Sue nodded. She was obviously not able to lead at this point, so once Wayne got back, they divided up the dead men's arms, goods, and personal effects.

Javor said, "I'll take point with Bixby, then Sue, Wayne, and Bruce who'll run the rear." Without even looking at Sue for agreement, he strode off with the next on-ramp the now smaller group's destination...

#####

Finn got the fresh milk out of the cooler, and placed it just so on the refreshment counter, and smiled at their luck. Not only had he been able to score the milk, but there was also a small carafe of fresh cream too.

It's the little things that we can get from the Farmer's guild, he thought, *that made life worth living again.*

At least it made the coffee taste so much better, he thought as he added a healthy dollop of cream to his coffee and went to join the other members of the Circle at the weekly meeting.

165

Vera, head of the Circle, was still sipping her coffee and smiling.

Good sign, Finn thought.

Maeve interrupted, of course, to get things started. "The fact that this Javor—the spaceman—is on his way, but we've not heard a thing? Seems like my own program, denied by this Circle for budgetary reasons, to populate the hinterland with more ham radio groups could have really helped out, now couldn't it?" she said primly.

Finn nodded—*and then realizing he was the only one doing so*, he shook his head instead.

No one seemed to notice, however, as Vera put down her coffee mug. "Thank the guild for the cream—milk too, please Finn," she said as she turned to face Maeve across the table.

"It was simple credits, Maeve, that put an end to your program. But yes, it would have helped to have gotten some kind of updates daily or even every other day from Sue and cadre. That said, their first stop will be at the Adair power station, and we can let them know to have Sue contact us then. Will that do?"

Maeve nodded and said, "Course, there's those dozens of miles across the Badlands to Lindos— then again up here to Arlington—that my program would have helped too," she said, and while no one at the table disagreed, her tone was almost a whine.

"We'll look at it next year, I promise," Vera said, and she clicked on her new tablet.

The Circle's tablet recovery mission down in Crandon had been a partial success, and the resulting find of two whole containers of new tablets had been eagerly taken up by the whole Regime. Techies were still working on the re-birth of the batteries, but some of the early ones had made it through to the Circle, and in front of each of them was a brand new tablet. All had been using them now for a couple of days, and it really did help to be wired in the Regime network at the same time. Saving and printing was easier. Messaging was quicker and discussions could go on between anyone who wanted to chat or conference too.

"Okay, we know more about this—what'd you call him, Maeve? A spaceman? Haven't heard that used in decades, but yes, this man who came down on the ... the *Drake*, I believe. We know a lot more —most importantly, that he has no real factual evidence that the Boathi are after him—or not. Nor, if the *Drake* will ever fly again. I'd like our own tech teams to look into that so we'd have a bunch of real testing queries for him when he arrives. That, and yes, I'd like our own techs to both visit and inspect the craft too, but that's in the future."

"And if the Boathi do show up? Before whomever might be on rescue duty for the Empire,

I mean?" Gemma asked, and that sent the discussion off on a new tangent.

"Would they even know that this ship is in need of a rescue?" Nixon asked.

"Would have to—the spaceman said that the ship's AI took over and jumped them twenty lights, and so it would have sent that back via Ansible—wouldn't it?" Harper asked, as she sipped her tea.

Vera nodded. "Like some of you, I too think that the Empire knows—and will be searching. Hard to say how much the Boathi will do too to find the , which would be good to know too. There are so many questions we don't have the answers for as yet—but as soon as this Javor gets here, we can ask and hopefully get real answers!"

Finn sipped his coffee and cream one more time and then cleared his throat. "Could I ask one thing? Is there any way that this spaceman—Javor, I mean —could be trouble for us? Didn't he say that one could just live in his ship and live well? Why then would he have left it is what I mean?"

That took them off on another tangent, and the talk centered around why sitting alone in a ship could ever be what one could call a good existence. No one thought that he'd been honest about that— but the fact that the ship had AI that was leading edge was something else to ponder.

"Our own AI is, what, eight years out of date?,"

Reid said, "and if we can get access to the AI on that ship and use it to add to our own—think of what that could mean to us all. AI that works better than all the issues we face. Not just to secure a home or building but to actively go out and mow down our enemies—that's something I'd like to see," he said forcefully.

That did get a nod or two.

Vera responded, "Reid, just because the dumb zombies try to eat us while their smarter cousins try to defeat us—it's not our place to ensure that they all die. They are the results of the Boathi virus bombs—so it's not them that we should hate, now is it?" she said, and her voice was polite but still meant to spell out her own point of view.

Reid shook his head. "My enemy is anyone who tries to kill me. End of story. So yes, they've all got to die. As do the sects we have met and been ambushed by, like various tribes and even some of the forest cliques too. We are the only humans still left on Bones—Ceti4, to be more precise. So we need to take back our world, I believe. Don't you all?" he finished off, and that got some more nods too.

Harper spoke up. "Yes, anyone that attacks me gets what they deserve. But say we could use the spaceman's AI to help us make an antidote for the zombies—dumb or smart. We could change them

back to being human say—is that not a better
answer than killing them all?"

More nods. A grunt too from Vera.

"Absolutely—but until we know more—this is
just talk. Intel is what we need, and that's for sure,"
she said as she made some notes on her tablet and
then went on to the next item on the Circle Agenda.

"It's called Walkerville for a reason," Bruce said
as he caught up with the group who'd stopped near
the off-ramp to the right with the sign pointing to
the town that lay to the north.

He smiled as the group stopped there and took a
breather. It'd been a dogged four miles since they'd
left the truck tank and their dead. No one had
talked, and while they'd made great time, what lay
behind them weighed heavily on their collective
minds.

Sue looked down the ramp, then crossed the
highway to look north, and after a few seconds
turned to them all.

"I think we can use a break, so let's do this. Let's
get off the interstate and into Walkerville. Let's see
if we can find a spot to take an afternoon off—wash,
relax, and just let the past twenty-four hours drift
away. Tomorrow, we'll be back right up here and
on our way—that suit you all?" she asked, and all of

them nodded.

"Uh … you do remember that Walkerville is called that because there's nothing there to enjoy, right, Sue, 'cause everyone walked away?" Bruce said with a raised eyebrow.

"Other than the old destroyed Ceti4 army barracks, this place is dead, right?"

"Old wives' tales," she answered. "Besides, that's what we want, right? A quiet empty place to take a breather, so let's go." Hoisting up her backpack, she took point and led the way down the off-ramp.

They passed a couple of cars. *One looked almost brand new,* Javor thought, and yet Bixby didn't bother with any of them. He trotted ahead to the bottom of the ramp where it curved slowly to the north and then out along the two lanes ahead of them. A half hour later found them going through an intersection with the charred remains of gas stations on all four corners.

Wayne grunted. "If all four of these made money, that'd be a surprise," he said.

Sue nodded. "No way that all four did—some were probably supported by the head office, I'd gather. Was the way back then, each had to face off against the others or else customers would think less of a brand. Least that's what I was told," she said as they all walked along the middle of the road going into town just ahead.

Not a lot of car hulks, Javor noted. *Nor trucks either for that matter.* As they slowly walked along, he kept one eye on Bixby who ambled ahead of them, but he also tried to look down the side streets too.

On one, there was a huge group of twisted cars and trucks—like someone had tossed them all into a pile that was fifty feet tall. He stopped and pointed.

Sue nodded. "See further a bit—on the left-hand side? See that crater there? Must have been a power substation, which got a direct Boathi hit. Destroyed the building and the power grid attached to same, I'd think, and moved the whole parking lot up into the air to come down like you see it. Seen lotsa these kind of piles—this one's pretty small too. You'll see what I mean when we get to the Adair Dam area ..." she finished off as they continued to walk into the small town ahead.

At one time, people had parked in what they once called angle parking when they visited what was once called downtown or the town core. Javor knew that from Gallipedia, and as they drew closer it was easy to see hulk after destroyed hulk of cars, pickups, and even some motorcycles. All were badly burned up and stripped of items, which was normal. When there was no manufacturing to make a new set of wiper blades, you took a set off another car. That's if you could siphon gas to run your own —and then after a few more years, as things broke, the skill to keep something on the road became harder to find.

Means, he thought, *that after eight years, there's nothing on the road anymore. Well, at least as far as I 've seen ...*

Ahead, Sue stopped and pointed down the side street to the left. "Let's take this one down to the old army barracks. Should be space there to camp out in, and good fencing as I remember from years ago on my first trip by here," she said and turned.

Bixby hastened to get ahead of her, and Javor moved up to take point with her, and Bruce and Wayne followed close behind.

As they walked, the number of houses on the quiet side street slowly decreased. Empty lots appeared and overgrown grass strips lined the cracked and disheveled street scape. One of the few remaining houses had been boarded up. There were sheets of plywood over all the doors and windows, and the front door had an iron gate in front of it.

"Seems like whoever lived there tried to stay," Javor said, and Sue nodded but could add no more.

As they left the few houses behind, the street became less like a town street. The sidewalks disappeared, the white line down the street center disappeared, and the undergrowth was taller than they were. After about a half mile more, on the right side of the street, the undergrowth suddenly disappeared too as there was now tarmac behind a tall frost fence that stretched away from them to their right and ahead of them for hundreds of yards to the abandoned army base.

Sue nodded and they moved toward what looked like an access point through the frost wire fencing and a guard shack too. At the doorway to same, she walked straight through, ignoring the skeletons that were piled in one corner. Bixby skirted them too, gingerly walked through the shack with them, and then ran ahead onto the army base road.

They all stood for a moment looking out at the buildings ahead: two- and three-story brick buildings that weren't in too bad shape. Some had some broken windows but most looked at least halfway decent, Javor thought.

An old well-overgrown set of railway tracks ran right in front of them, leading off somewhere to the left.

Sue pointed at the building ahead. "This is admin —just offices. We need to go right here, around the tan building, and then back down that road to get to the barracks where we can rest and take it easy. Been there last time, and it's safe to rest there," she said and walked ahead of the group toward the tan building.

At the edge of same, she stopped and then looked across the base road to a side building that was much larger than any they'd seen so far. Big enough to be an aircraft hangar, a wall along this side was marked Motor Pool. The doors of the double doorway ahead swung in the breeze. It looked like someone had driven a truck right through them from the inside, as the top hinges of the doors were completely missing.

She pulled out her rifle immediately and took off the safety. The rest of the group grew more cautious and looked around slowly.

Bixby, however, just trotted down the base road toward the doors, and even though Javor whistled to him to return, he didn't pause but went in the open doors. Javor charged toward the same doors, and all of them were soon there at the doorway.

Inside, lying on the floor of the building about fifty feet away, Bixby was sitting in a pile of cardboard boxes and chewing something. In fact, as they all entered and spread out safely, Javor could see that those cardboard boxes were food boxes. Processed retail grocery store boxes. Boxes that couldn't have been made since eight years ago. Boxes that shouldn't exist today.

Around them stretching off for at least another hundred yards or so, there were all kinds of trucks parked in neat orderly rows—probably more than a hundred of them, Javor thought. *Some were definitely army trucks, the dull green and camo tops easy to identify. Others were retail delivery trucks with smiling customers grinning from the side. Some advertised some kind of cookie, two thin black rings around a white icing center. Others had families in their cars, snacking on some kind of a chip. Besides these trucks were a couple of large eighteen-wheelers,* Javor thought they were called, *with plain tarps protecting whatever cargo they carried or had carried.*

Interspersed with the trucks were huge dollies on casters with big bins to carry something, and they all walked slowly toward the trucks.

A few, they noticed as they glanced in, carried more of those retail food packs. Javor picked up a couple and noted that one said it was the best soup for a cold, and the other more rectangular box offered up that it held oat bran granola. Both were in perfect order. Both were filled with something, and as he tossed the soup box back into the bin, he opened up the granola bar box. Inside were eight foil-wrapped bars. He took one, and with his teeth, he tore a side off. Smiling at Sue who was trying to preach caution, he took a bite.

Granola, yes.

Still fit to eat, yes.

Good tasting—well, as good as granola ever was—yes.

He looked down at the box and searched for a best before date, and yes, there it was.

Best before more than eight years ago—yet here it was

still edible.

And not decayed and rotting.

Sue said it first.

"This is plenty odd—but I suspect we've just discovered where that Interstate Tribe of women do their shopping," she said, and then she wandered off to look around further.

Javor called for Bixby, finished another bite of the granola bar, and tossed the rest to his dog. Bixby caught it deftly in his mouth and then spit it out on the floor of the hangar. He bent down to sniff it one more time and then moved away.

"Guess the dog don't like granola," Javor said to himself with a grin, and he soon caught up with Sue.

In front of the first line of trucks to their left, there were huge doors—interior doors it looked like—that lead somewhere else, but each was closed and didn't appear like it could be forced open either.

They searched for a way in and didn't find a single way to gain access to what lay behind that wall of sealed doors. Bruce had just completed a lap around the whole of the interior of the hangar, and he got back a bit out of breath.

"Sue, nothing else at all. Trucks on the hangar floor, those sealed doors, and dollies haphazardly around the floor. Not a thing else," he said, and they all looked at each other, stymied.

"Some did have their keys hanging from the ignition switches, I saw," he added.

"Take anything that you figure you'd eat," Sue said "and let's find some bunks—I'm done with today."

After some digging, Javor grabbed a box of crackers shaped like animals, and he smiled at that.

Moving back to the open doors, he stopped and took a look.

"Someone sawed the locking mechanism, then drove outta here, I'd guess" he said, as he saw fresh saw marks on the locking arm.

"Good to know, but as far as the Regime told me last time—my only time here I should add—this place is deserted—Walkerville is deserted.

They all fell into the same group as they went out of the building and then turned once again to their right to go down the base side road and toward the rows of single-story barracks coming up on their left. Sue led the way past the first and second barracks and went right to the third one. Bixby didn't like something, Javor thought, as he was walking stiff-legged on the walkway between the rows of barracks buildings and growled occasionally.

"Let's be cautious here," Javor said, "Bixby isn't happy ..."

"Third one is lucky," Sue said, "as that's the one

I was in before." She trotted up the few stairs to the doorway and threw back the screen door at the same time as the inner door opened up and zombie hands stretched out for her just inches away ...

She stuck her gun into the doorway and pulled the trigger twice. As she fell backward off the stoop, Bruce's gun sounded from behind them, and more and more zombies fell, clogging the doorway.

Javor leaned forward to Sue's arm, and he helped drag her off the stoop to the left, while Wayne and Bruce fired continuously into the barracks interior.

"Lots of them," Bruce yelled, as Sue got back up to her feet and retreated with the rest of the group as they poured volley after volley into the third barracks building.

From across the walkway to their right, zombies poured out of the barracks that lay there as well as from the two barracks they'd passed over initially.

Sue said, "Back to the hangar—we'd have only one doorway for them to get to us."

Retreating slowly, firing and reloading, they made it to the hangar, and Javor noted Bixby was ahead of them once more.

#####

Moving quickly, faster than a zombie, was always possible, the group knew, and they quickly ran back to the Motor Pool building. Bruce moved past the other three who stood in the doorway ready to fight right there and pushed a big dolly with a half-full bin of food items into the opening. Wayne nodded and helped. In one minute, the entire open doorway was a mass of dollies jammed together, stopping any access.

"Could still crawl over, one by one," Sue said, "but that'd take brainpower a dumb zombie doesn't have."

She helped Wayne drag a smaller dolly up to sit by the others. They quickly flipped it over and then climbed on top, which gave them a height advantage as they could now see the stumbling slow zombies appear and turn toward the Motor Pool.

Each seemed to be unable to understand what it was they faced, Javor noted, as they simply walked up to the dollies and then stopped. Not one tried to push the dollies out of their way—or what would have been even better, drag them outward and away from the doorway.

As more and more arrived, Sue said, "About thirty or so" and even that large a group couldn't muster how to get into the building.

"Thinking we're good here," Wayne said as he put the safety back onto his rifle and smiled.

And he appeared to be right, Javor noted, and only then did he turn to bark "No" to Bixby who'd been howling behind them.

Seeing the trucks behind him again made him wonder why they were here. And why they had been left behind.

"If you were going to move a whole bunch of food into some kind of storage, you'd need trucks, right?" he asked no one.

Sue nodded and Bruce said, "Right."

"So when the time comes to get those items outta storage, you'd need trucks again, right?"

That got him an answering nod from Sue.

"And while we did see gas stations just downtown, I'd say that a real army type, attention to detail type, would make sure that their trucks are gassed and ready to go. Right?" he asked as he began to walk over to a truck that was close.

"Right again, Javor—are you thinking that these things will start? Oh—and you do know that we've all," Sue said as she looked at both Wayne and Bruce, "have never ever even driven a truck before too, right?" she said dryly.

"But I have—ain't hard," he answered as he opened up the truck with the cookie advertisement on its side and hoisted himself up the two external steps into the cab and into the left-hand driver's seat leaving the door open.

Steering wheel type of vehicle, he noted, and he'd used that kind before, but the stick was so much easier. Dash had gauges and some kind of display unit that was a black unpowered screen now. It had no rear mirror, but two big unbroken side mirrors showed the sides of the truck all the way back to the next row of army trucks. Down on the driver's side of the floorboards were the two pedals he knew he'd need—gas and brake. Don't know which is which yet, but good to see he'd had a bit of experience with this kind of truck.

Keys. Trucks needed keys or security thumbprint readers or AI that was up and running.

He said, "AI, new driver help, please," and waited.

Nothing. If AI was up and running, he'd not gotten an answer, as there must be something else he needed to add.

He looked at the steering column and yes—there was a place to insert a key. Least must be the place, he thought. Now all he needed to do was to find the key. The full bench seat beside him held nothing. He leaned way over to his right and saw that the truck had a special compartment. He grabbed the lift handle and it popped open. No keys. There were papers about some kind of service that the truck had had before the bombs had fallen, but nothing more.

He sighed. *He'd have to check each of them.* He remembered Bruce had said he'd found some with keys, as he straightened up and looked up. Above the driver's and passenger's side of the windshield were some kind of flaps with paperwork jammed in behind them. He brushed down the one on the driver's side, and from behind them, a set of keys fell into his lap.

"*Bingo!*" he said to himself and smiled. "Need to remember that keys are often tucked away up there."

He looked at the key ring—three keys. One was much bigger and he thought that it would be for the rear locking cargo area.

But the other two were the same key, and he smiled as he inserted it slowly into the key socket on the steering column and gave it a hard twist the only way it'd go.

Vroom! Vroom!

The truck started on the first turn and ran loud and rough, but he could still see Sue and the others jumping up and down.

They had a truck that they could use!

The trip ahead to Arlington just got much shorter.

He played with the pedal on the left and nothing happened, but the one on the right increased the flow of fuel as the truck engine revved as he did that, and eventually the rough idle quieted down.

Fuel. Trucks need fuel that they carry themselves.

He studied the dash display one more time, and in the bottom left-hand corner, he found a gauge that read Fuel Gauge on the top, and below it a red line was centered over the letter F.

F is for full, he hoped. *But no way to tell how much fuel that was nor how far it'd get them.*

He turned the truck off.

Sue clapped him on the back as he got down, and he smiled and then stopped the congratulations. Even Wayne standing over near the doorway on the overturned dolly doing his watchman role smiled and gave him a thumbs up!

"Wait," he said, "wait … we'll need to take a truck that has full fuel and somehow make sure of that," he said.

Bruce nodded. "A couple of them army trucks— back over there," he said as he pointed well away from where they were standing, "had like rows and rows of what looked like some kind of containers— red ones, I think," he said.

Bruce and Javor trotted over to take a look-see. At one of those army trucks, there were at least fifty of those red plastic containers. Javor opened one up and took a smell.

"Gas. They're all full of gas, so we need to take some of these with us," he said and then had a sudden thought as he turned to Sue.

"Moving across Bones in a truck is going to cause

us some real attention. Do we want to identify ourselves as army—by taking one of their trucks, or maybe we just move the gas cans into a food truck and folks might think we have cookies?"

Not knowing what the politics of this kind of statement would mean on Bones was an issue, and as he stood and scratched Bixby's ear, Sue and Bruce talked it out.

They'd take a non-army vehicle, loaded with gas was their decision.

He smiled and began to walk the rows of food trucks. One had an advertisement for something called Nutty Spread with a picture of a couple of kids spreading dark goop on bread. When he reached that smaller truck, he looked inside and smiled.

"Keys in the ignition, bench seat up front, crew cab behind, and the back is empty. Let me just check that she starts," he said, and on the third twist of the key, the engine fired right up. As he studied the dash, he saw that the word FULL appeared on the display in this truck, and that was a good start. Meanwhile, Sue and Bruce had carried more than two dozen of those red fuel cans over and jammed them in the back.

"Not much room for more—at least where they won't roll around, I mean, 'cause we got them all braced up with some of the truck's cargo itself,"

Bruce said.

Javor nodded. He told them to get in, and then he slowly pulled the truck out of the row it was in and turned to his left.

Moving toward the piled-up dollies, he stopped long enough to get Wayne into the cab after he closed the vertical rear door, and he looked at everyone.

"We're going straight out. I'm turning left toward the gate, and then I'll cut across the grass, over the tracks, and then left out the huge hole in the fence, back to Walkerville. Okay with that?"

"We got time to get a pool on how many zombies you run over," Wayne said with a smile, and everyone laughed.

Javor gunned the engine.

She ran fine, he thought, as he slowly pushed up against the dollies that quickly rolled out of his way as he left the building. Zombies too were moved mostly outward and away, but some did fall, and yet he didn't feel that bad about them. They'd kill me if they had a chance.

At the edge of the road, he spun the wheel to the left as Sue sitting beside him grabbed his arm and pointed back to the right toward the barracks area they'd just left.

Down about a hundred yards stood some more zombies—but they were neatly dressed, Javor thought. They were standing still and watching the truck. They were talking among themselves and Sue nodded.

"Ah, the smart zombies who're running this base," she surmised and waved him on.

Javor turned the wheel more sharply, goosed the truck, and left the base behind ... over the grass, through the fence, and back toward Walkerville.

CHAPTER SEVEN

Climbing back up the off-ramp had been no problem at all for the truck. It made the climb easily yet he had to use a three-point turn to get going back to the east up top. They were calling the truck Nutty because of the advertisement on the side, and they were asking him to boot it so that they could go faster. He'd reminded them three times that fuel was their major concern and slow and steady would make their supply last longer. Bruce griped about that and said that at least once every ten miles or so, he should get her up to fifty miles an hour and that got support, but Javor nixed that idea. Bruce and Wayne, who sat behind in the crew cab area with Bixby sitting up between them, grumbled.

Sue nodded and agreed.

Fuel longevity was something to be concerned with, so

that was that.

Still, on some miles of the interstate ahead, where the roads had been clean and garbage free, he did get her up to about forty or so, and that made the miles and scenery fly by.

Off to the north was the start of the rolling hills leading to the mountains from which that nor'wester had come, while down to their right, the southern landscape was totally different. Here, the valleys opened up and farm after farm and woodlot after woodlot were all they could see. Smaller county roads were covered with gravel and sometimes a wreckage of cars and trucks too. At one point, Bruce said, "Hey, look at all them tractors" when they passed a small town with a tractor dealership. Parked in rows like soldiers on parade, the tractors' orange paint was still shiny in the late afternoon sun.

"What's ahead?" Javor asked Sue, who stopped staring at the interstate scenery and nodded to him.

"Sign back there said nine miles to Adair, which is a smaller town like Maxwell, off to the north. We gotta get off the interstate to not miss it, then go north through town to the river, and then upriver about another five miles to the Adair Dam. Once we're there, the power station will know early as they'll surely hear Nutty coming, and we'll get entry into their grounds. Fully fortified and protected too ... so no zombies either and won't be using these," she said as she patted her rifle that lay beside her.

Javor grunted and watched the roadway ahead. Twice, he slowed a bit more to twist the truck across the three lanes to avoid car and truck pileups, and once, Bruce, Wayne, and Sue had to get out to wrestle some timber and beams off the one lane so that he could get through there too. Ahead, the interstate was pretty clear, and he gunned it all the way up to almost sixty and had the boys and Sue laughing at such speeds.

He grinned. *Might have cost us a cup of gasoline, but the hell with it.*

At the the off-ramp ahead, the sign read Town of Adair, and he angled the truck over to the right to slow and look down first.

Blocked.

There had been a big smashup of vehicles — trucks and what looked like a whole raft of those orange tractors on a carrier too. There was no way that Nutty would get by, and he told them so and backed up to go ahead to the on-ramp.

Once there, again he had to use a three-point turn to face back to the west, but it was clear at least, and down he went slowly, the truck mostly rolling on its own. At the bottom, he rolled right on through the intersection, around two cars and over the curb, and then took a hard right to get underneath the interstate. As the truck went on, Javor moved it carefully around the occasional vehicle still on the road and reached the next large intersection ahead. There, Sue said, "Take a right," and he did that. They slowly went down the regional road toward the town still miles ahead.

On the south side, the interstate continued its one hundred feet in the air and the valley lay below as the regional roadway slowly climbed the rolling hills to Adair.

On the north side sat a few farms, woodlots, and even a gas station too, which had been almost burned to the ground. In the far distance, Javor saw what looked like a school with several buses lined up outside.

After less than another hundred feet, Bruce asked him to stop for a moment. He did so, and as he turned to ask why, he saw that Bruce had opened up his door and was standing on the door sill, looking off to the left of the truck. Javor was about to ask why when the sound of Bruce's rifle exploded twice.

Bam! Bam!

And then Bruce got back into the rear seat.

"Zombies and now there's two less," he said, "but before you all give me hell, I had to just test the sights once more after that dang ambush back in

Walkerville. Sorry," he offered.

Sue grunted and said, "Let's go."

Javor did just that but asked, "How far away were those two, Bruce?"

"Sights have various pre-sets, and that was at 300 yards—accurate too—I like this weapon," he added.

Javor grunted. Three hundred yards is like three throws of my javelin. He sighed and went back to watching carefully for the road and anything in their way.

"Okay," Sue said, "here, we gotta go to the left." She pointed left ahead where the regional road split at a T-intersection.

Javor negotiated that, and the truck slowly climbed the grade ahead for almost a half mile as the town of Adair rose up ahead. He looked and watched carefully as they crept along at ten miles an hour. An hour ago, he'd realized that the truck had only the four tires that were on it—there were no spares—and if he'd been thinking a bit better back at the Motor Pool, he'd have tried to find some spares to toss in the back too. But he hadn't and so he watched the road ahead with a higher degree of caution than he'd planned. Least the cadre members hadn't thought of that too, so far. He half-smirked to himself, and as the truck crept up the final bit of grade at the top of the last intersection coming into town, he stopped in the middle of same.

"So, this is Adair," he said and was not impressed.

Again, the town had angle parking on both sides of the main street ahead—downtown he would call it. It really wasn't much of a city center. Some of the cars were just empty hulks, while a couple looked fairly nice still. Two orange tractors sat askew on a stage on the left with a torn and ratty banner advertising the big draw to win them at the upcoming Fall Fair—but that was from eight years ago. Someone had broken almost every single window in town, and someone else had torched the big diner on the street corner too. Part of the frontage of a five-and-dime store was hanging down onto the wide sidewalk area with hundreds and hundreds of books lying there too.

Wonder who's gonna read them, Javor thought.

"Not much of a town, but then eight years after the Boathi, guess we're all lucky just to see it," Sue said ruefully, and they all nodded.

Javor put the truck back into drive and moved ahead, taking a cautious path down the center of the main drag. He was careful to try to avoid the big pile of glass that was ahead too. Looks like someone had sat and looked at those tractors and drank a whole boatload of beer—and then had smashed the empties right there too. Two patio chairs were still set up to face the stage, and Javor wondered if he could sit and look back those years and not break the empties either. Nope, couldn't do that either. He drove around the big brown smashed bottles and went farther down the street.

What he thought was the town's city hall was ahead of them. It was an older style of architecture and made from nice gray rock with some columns out front, but the dome above had fallen into disrepair and had holes in its shell. On the front lawn—or what might have been lawn years ago—lay dozens of skeletons. All were lying with remnants of some kind of body bags dissolved around them. All, he figured, had been deposited there when the virus bombs fell and the collection of bodies had begun.

He shook his head and raised an eyebrow at Sue.

She nodded. "We were told that, yeah, when the first virus victims were killed, that you had to take your dead in yourself to the authorities so that they could then test them to see from what it was they'd died. Not 'til everyone started to die within a month or two more, did someone not bother as the lab guys who were to do the testing started dying and so here they lay," she said.

Sad that this still lay in tribute to what the Bones governments had tried to do—but had failed—as the Boathi virus bombs had been so successful.

He drove on farther past what looked like the

perfectly okay post office, past the big department store, and two motor hotels too, the signs stated. He followed the road as it jogged to first the left and then the right, past a big box store parking lot with hundreds of vehicles all neatly parked. He looked past them to the stores themselves, and while he didn't recognize any of the brand names, he knew what a shoe store or a home decoration store looked like, and he just shook his head.

Sue pointed at the next intersection and said, "Take a right here, all the way out to the edge of town to the power substation."

He nodded and in less than five minutes, the truck eased up at the securely locked front gate of the Adair power station. "More than a football field big," he said to himself, "fully fenced with huge transformers and rows of marching towers that held the current wires and moved the power elsewhere."

He knew enough to note that there didn't appear to be any incoming power lines, but he could easily identify the lightning arresters, the enormous step-down transformer, and the voltage regulators. That he'd learned about them more than thirty years ago or so back on his home world during a summer job meant little now—but this station did have the hum he'd always heard when power was being controlled, and that meant someone ran this station.

Sue asked, "Does Nutty have a horn?"

He grinned at her and pressed down hard on the center of the steering wheel.

BEEP ... BEEP ... BEEP!

And then they waited.

From a small building ahead, three men exited, and two carried rifles pointed generally in their direction.Sue said, "Let me get this," opened up the door, and stepped down, unarmed.

She held up her hands, palms toward the three men who were now standing still only thirty feet away but behind the big fence gate, and said, "Hello—we're from Maxwell—we're with the Regime." She stood still to let them look at her.

One of the men spoke to the other two, and the three men walked up to cut the distance down between them and Sue.

"Easy to say—can we ask if we contact the Regime on ham radio that you have a code that they'd accept?" one asked, his hands just tucked into his belt. About thirty years old, he had a big bushy ginger beard. He wore boots, rough jeans, and a matching jean jacket.

"Can we see everyone, please? Plus the truck? Where did you find a working vehicle?" he asked, and while he took care with his question, Javor could tell the truck was more important than they were.

Sue nodded and waved at them all, and everyone

left their arms in the truck and got out. Javor did not bother to remove his Colt so it sat on his hip, but the three men ahead either didn't notice or didn't care. One of them, he noted though, pointed his rifle a bit closer to him, and that made sense, even if it was uncomfortable.

Sue said, "Yes, our code is Maxwell four, twenty-five, ninety-three—the day the bombs fell. Please send that over ham radio, and we'll wait.

One of the men ahead pointed behind the truck, said something, and the lead power station man, the ginger, said, "You're pulling in a crowd, so let's get you through the gate first, okay?" as he motioned behind them.

Javor turned to look, and coming down the road still quite a bit back were zombies. Dumb zombies, it appeared, but at least a couple of dozen, and as he turned back, Sue nodded and he hoisted himself back up into the cab of the truck.

One of the three power station men went over to a panel on a wall inside the fence, and the huge gate ahead of them powered up and slid out of the way.

Driving the truck inside was easy, and he put it down the road and off to one side where the other power station fellow indicated. Javor climbed out of the truck along with Bixby who'd been asleep.

He barked once and then was quiet as Javor threw him a whole jerky bar, and he gnawed on that.

The leader spoke. "A truck—a working truck. A dog. Code that will validate you too perhaps—are there any other surprises you might have?" he asked.

They all turned to walk back toward the big building that was off to one side of the substation, and Javor wondered *what the man would think if he were to say that yes, he wasn't from Bones either ... but best to let Sue decide that one.*

Bixby wasn't a happy camper when he was put in the back of the truck so that one of the power substation men could accompany them the few more miles to the dam itself. He kept up a longish story of what the issues were at the dam and how the penstock needed cleaning every three months and how the extra spillway that those goddamn Boathi bombs had missed should'a been hit too.

All in all, the story was what anyone would hear from workers anywhere on any kind of job, Javor thought.

Sue smiled every so often when she'd say something like "No, really?" or even "Tell me what that is?"

As the truck slowly climbed the narrow two-lane road carved right out of the side of the small mountain ahead, the river below them ran fast with

large ripples and sprays from rocks along the
watercourse. That recent nor'wester had come
down with so much rain that the river was running
brown where the current was the slowest—silt,
mud, and dirt all washing down from the massive
storm.

The side of the mountain above the road was
thick with fir trees that rose all the way to the top.
The thick forests had not been trimmed or looked
after as the road often had small piles of scrub and
fall-downs that were merely pushed off the narrow
lanes of the road.

The lightning from that storm had also struck a
few of the tallest trees, and some still smoldered
with black sooty smoke. The rain from the storm
must have been just enough to prevent a forest fire.

Road maintenance was obviously something that
wasn't a priority, Javor thought, as he carefully
threaded the truck around the piles and kept slowly
climbing the slope of the road ahead of them.

At the top of the next rise, the road angled down
and to the right a bit, and they could see the dam.
Or maybe what was left of the dam would be a
better way to think of the view ahead. The Boathi
bombs had fallen right on target it looked like, as
the height of the dam had been cut down by at least
a hundred feet. What was left of the dam that was
not blown up stretched across the six hundred feet

of river it held back, and it still did that just fine. Where there had been six spillways in the major part of the dam, only concrete rubble and debris remained. From where the truck sat above the dam, Javor could see one spillway off to the far right was full of river water pouring down into the generating plant area.

Even from this far away, Javor could see, *something was wrong at the far right of the spillway.*

As he slipped the truck into low, to take it easy down the hill, he saw a big mass of fallen floating fir trees that seemed to be caught at the edge of that far spillway. Above that mass of needles and branches, a large, long crane stretched out to sit right above that area, coming from the dam grounds maintenance area. Next to that, he could just see a small inflatable boat caught by the spillway metal grates too, its outboard tossing up a big rooster tail as it went nowhere but stayed off to one side, caught by another of those trees.

The truck hit a couple of ruts, and Bixby barked loudly as he got tossed about a bit, but Javor still went ahead at a greater speed than he first thought prudent. Sue could now see the turmoil below and she egged him on.

I know little about dams, he thought, but enough to know that the rushing water spins a turbine that is hooked up to a generator that generates electricity and moves it to a transformer and then out to power lines. And spillways that lead the water to the turbines have metal grates to protect the equipment from logs and the like.

"Least that's what happens on a real dam — perhaps not one that has been hit by the Boathi," he said to himself.

At the bottom of the slope, they turned a hard right at another high frost wire fence gate, and a couple of men came running out and one of them whistled.

"Wow, a truck! A real live moving truck," he said and whistled yet again.

"We've got issues here — two men are caught in the spillway grates," the second one said, as they turned back to run the hundred yards across the top of the dam and to the area directly under the crane.

As soon as he could, Javor parked and turned off the truck. He pressed the open tailgate button that would free Bixby and got out of the cab to run to the area himself. He was followed by the others ,and when Sue arrived, she yanked on one of the men's coat sleeves and said, "Effram — it's me, Sue, from Maxwell ... can we help?"

"Sue, right? We met here about four years ago, when you and some others came for a tour — I'm Effram Howey — the boss up here at the dam. And we've got troubles but no way out of same yet," he explained.

The big nor'wester had taken down many trees well up river, and when they came up to the dam, most could be lifted up and over and tossed downriver by the crane. Most. But a few had gotten stuck in the metal cage crates that protected their one working dam spillway. The branches were wedged into the square holes in the grate and wouldn't let go. When the crane was attached to the trees, it only broke off branches as the two trees were now jammed into the grates together. The trees were enormous—at least a hundred feet tall.

Effram and his crew had launched their inflatable boat with the outboard figuring that the two men could help by getting a better lock on the central bole of the top tree so the crane could successfully lift it out of the way. They'd tried locking the big hawser onto the bole and then had backed off as the crane lifted and lifted, and the top tree jammed in on the other had begun to move. It had moved slowly up and up and then the hawser had let go … and the tree had fallen back down but was now ten or so feet higher up.

He shook his head then.

"And then I made a mistake—I okayed that the boat go back and retry to hook up the hawser. The boys did and the tree shifted when they were right under it, and its branches grabbed the side of the inflatable, and both of them hit the water. That's Billy out there in the gray life jacket clutching the top of that damn tree, and Tony just a bit off beside him in the orange life jacket. And the boat is stuck but they can't get to it 'cause it's off to that one side."

He shook his head one more time.

"We need to get our men back safely — which is why we're working on getting the crane extension hooked up," he said as he pointed behind him with his thumb.

Everyone turned to look up on the roof of the generator building. A whole crew of workmen was involved in the dismantling of the rear end of the crane assembly, and they could see thirty-foot extension of the crane boom beside it on a set of pallets.

"How long 'til that can be completed and tested?" Sue asked.

"Dunno about the testing part, but it'll be at least an hour," Effram answered.

From where they stood, the two men out holding onto the top of the tree looked like they weren't doing so well.

"Water temp after the nor'wester would be ..." Sue asked.

"Down," Effram responded. "She's probably at around forty to fifty degrees. They've been out there, what, forty minutes already.

"Don't mean to ask ..." Sue said.

"An hour at forty degrees is your answer," Effram answered.

They all knew that meant the two men out there had less than twenty minutes or so before deep hypothermia began to set in. One of the first things to go was the ability to hold on to things like tree branches. The men would slowly lose their ability to keep above the water level and slide down and into the cold, cold water.

"We gotta get them out of there soon," Effram said, wringing his hands together.

Javor spoke up. "Could I ask—how far out exactly is that boat?"

Effram looked over at him and said, "Why?"

"Looks to me like it's about fifty, maybe fifty-five, feet out there. Is that what you'd think?" he went on.

Effram took a few steps to his right and held out a hand to gaze directly at the concrete spillway sluice rail that lay out about the same distance as the boat.

"That sluice rail—see it—the concrete arm that juts out into the river that curls the water toward the spillway down below? She's exactly sixty feet out there from the shoreline to the tip of same. And the crane is only setup for forty feet right now," he finished off.

Javor nodded and began to take off his armored vest, his Colt, and other gear, and placed them all in a pile.

"You can't swim out there—the current will rip you down into the spillway, and the turbines will cut you in two," Effram said, holding out his hand.

"Ain't gonna swim," Javor said. "I'm just gonna jump out to the boat," he answered, and that got a puzzled look from everyone.

Sue shook her head and held out an arm to bar his way. "Javor—that's like fifty feet or so. No one can jump that far—you'll fall into the water and get sucked down into the spillway tunnel and die. You do see that, right?" she said.

"Most people, yes. But I guess I neglected to mention that I was a decathlon winner a couple of decades ago and the long jump was my specialty. That, and as I've had my whole right knee rebuilt with alien tissue and technology, I used to hit fifty-feet jumps all the time. Well, at least a couple," he said, and he was only fibbing by maybe five feet.

He had won the long jump with forty-eight feet when he was thirty-one those long years ago. "A couple of feet more he could do easy, right?" he said to himself as he moved along the shoreline to check the path for his approach run.

The edge of the dam itself was smooth concrete at

the very edge with only a small two-inch up-curl at the water's edge.

He placed his foot there and took twenty-two strides back at a perfectly perpendicular path, and he drew a line there on the concrete with his heel.

He had gathered quite a small group of bystanders, and he told them to stay out of that pathway to give him some security for the jump.

He knew he had to slap down his right foot flat, right up tight to that up-curl of concrete to launch himself up at less than twenty degrees to get the vertical impulse of his own center of gravity right. To maintain balance and control, he also knew, as he'd done this jump tens of thousands of times, he would then push back on his left arm to counterweight the right leg push off and fully extend that arm too.

He knew all of this, as he stretched and bounced on his right leg, warming up the alien tissue in his knee.

No troubles with same since the nor'wester either. Not a single spasm or the like either.

He grinned to himself. Of course, that might be because the right knee had been in a truck for the last two days instead of hiking along the interstate.

He got ready and then realized that once he hit the boat, he had no plan, so he waved Effram and Sue over.

"And when I land in the boat—she's a standard

outboard, right?

"Right," Effram said. "Just run her up, get the two of them to climb aboard, and then take off directly across the river to the far side. We'll have someone there to meet you." He turned to bark orders to the crews around him.

Javor looked at Sue who was the only one now in front of him.

"You can do this, right?" she asked with a look on her face that said she hoped so.

He just nodded. "Can of corn," he added and then waved her out of his way.

Out in the water, the man in the gray life jacket was slipping off the treetop, and he knew it was time.

He flexed his legs, doing a couple of deep knee bends—the right one felt great.

He turned to face totally away from the dam, said a small thanks to the alien who'd provided his tissue, and then turned and sprinted down the path directly at the edge of the dam.

He counted his steps as he knew when he got to the last two of them, how he stepped off those two would be the success or failure of his jump.

Eighteen.

Nineteen.

Twenty—and he ensured that his focus was down at his feet as he placed step twenty-one a single bound short of the edge of the dam.

Twenty-one—and he moved his right foot forward at breakneck speed as he slapped it down totally flat on the edge of the dam just short of the up-curl of concrete. Throwing back his left arm to be straight, he launched himself into the air.

Twenty-two—and his body remembered what it had known for decades.

He sailed, feet outstretched. Out and out and over the darkly roiling water below him.

Out and out and still going up as he tucked his body into a V shape, legs still going up.

Out and out and now no longer up but heading down toward the water below.

As he focused on the water as it got closer and closer, the edge of the inflatable began to jut into his eyesight, but he ignored it for a whole second. His legs were still ahead of the rest of his body, but he was slowly flexing his abdominals to force his body more upright.

Down. Down and as his butt hit the water, the side of the boat slammed him in the chest, and he grabbed it with all his might.

The water below tried to seize him and move him downward toward the spillway, but he wrestled with the side of the boat, happy that the designers had added a set of rope cleats to the sides. As he grabbed that yellow rope, he pulled his now cold legs out from under the boat, hoisted them over the side, and fell in.

The cheers from the shore were huge, but before he could rise to acknowledge same, he knew he had to get the two dam workers. He was shivering and getting colder himself, but he crawled down the short floor and took the seat at the helm in the rear.

His hands were freezing, so he jammed them under his armpits and squeezed them for a minute to get them warm so he could feel things again.

He looked at the tiller on the boat and saw that it was in forward, but a big sheaf of fir branches was jammed between the seat and the throttle. He ripped them out and threw them overboard, and the boat quit moving about at random. He twisted the throttle again, in neutral. The gas fed well, and he looked ahead at the two dam workers.

Orange jacket was closest, so he eased the boat into forward and then threaded a path through the mess of fir trees ahead. He got hung up on something below and had to rev the hell outta the outboard in reverse to get free, but in a minute he was sidling up to the orange-jacketed worker, and he dumped it into neutral again.

"Guess you're Tony—let me help you in," he said as he grabbed the man by the scruff of his jacket and slowly rolled the man backward and up and over the soft gunwales to lie in the boat bottom. No time to even talk to this, one but as he slid back up and onto the helm seat, Tony waved at him and clasped his legs to try to conserve warmth.

He put her in forward again and moved the boat around one more tree to where the gray-jacketed worker was—and the man was gone. No gray jacket to see. He rammed the boat into the tree at once, thinking that maybe it had slid down more into the spillway as the strong river current forced it down—but there was no—wait, he could see the gray jacket just below that side branch.

Javor jammed the throttle on full speed, and the boat slowly pushed and pushed against the treetop. Suddenly, the worker popped up, out of the clutches of the tree, and Javor grinned as he saw the worker trying to swing his arms to swim.

He put the boat in neutral, and with a bit of help from Tony, they both manhandled Billy on board too. He pushed the two of them into each other's arms to try to generate some warmth, and then in forward once more, he steered the boat away from the spillway feeder area and across the river.

He didn't much care about depth, as he got close, and he ran the inflatable right up on shore and was met with more workers than he thought would be at the dam. They hustled Tony and Billy off the boat, onto stretchers, and back toward wherever their sick bay was, and he smiled.

Just a jump and some boat work too.

Sue grinned at him on the shore, and Bixby barked twice too.

"So, now we've got a hero who can, like, jump almost across the whole bloody river," she said, and Wayne who'd just run up laughed right out loud.

"Boys look okay so far, and they're getting the hot towel treatment too," he said.

"Sleep, all I wanna do is to have a nap," Javor said as he slowly got up and out of the boat.

Sue clasped him around the shoulders and walked with him all the way back to the administration building.

"They gave us this room for our use—so the couch is yours for a few hours anyway," she said as she smiled at him.

Javor nodded. The knee was a bit stiff. Too much asked for too seldom was the problem. Still, couldn't have been for a better purpose, he thought.

He tucked his left arm under the pillow as he cautiously placed his right leg directly on top of his left and noted that Bixby had also come in to sit at the side of the couch.

"Sleep ... sleep is always good," he said to himself as his right knee pulsed and the waves of pain began to subside.

#####

Four hours later, Effram knocked on the door, and Bruce let him in.

"And you all are ..." he said, and Sue did the names all around.

When she got to Javor, who she saved for last, she sort of shrugged and said in a tone that reminded one of a tall tale.

"And this is Javor Novak—our spaceman. True story—he landed here on Bones only a few weeks back, and it's our job to get him to the Regime HQ in Arlington as soon as possible. And the dog is his too—Bixby is the pup's name—and he's a godsend when it comes to finding out what's ahead of us on the road—when we're walking, I mean. Truck we found back in Walkerville, and she's a godsend too, and we expect to be in Arlington now much sooner."

Effram nodded and held out his hand. "Well, that, and he can jump too. Jump far enough to help us out too. Tony is fine, and Billy will need another day or so on light duty, but yeah, Javor, many, many thanks."

He nodded and held out a hand to shake, and Javor did just that remembering that Bones citizens liked the use of personal touch to reinforce their feelings.

Effram smiled at him again. "Spaceman, eh? Then good to meet you and welcome to Bones—

well, Ceti4 really, but we all use Bones 'cause she's got good ones. We just need to help rebuild the planet—which is what we do here at the Adair Dam. We push power out every single second to the lines. Tour?" he asked suddenly and turned to lead the way.

Guess one can't say no, Javor thought, and he fell into line to make their way across the administration building and down a long hallway that was plain gray concrete. It angled down and down and then leveled out and stretched ahead. At the end of that long corridor, there was a large open three-story-high room. In the middle of it ran a row of generators all topped with huge transformers sitting unpowered—they obviously had been put out of working order by the Boathi bombs eight years ago. But at the very end, the last generator was running and humming and, yes, probably generating power as the transformer was humming too. As they went by, they waved at the two workers who were tending the unit and continued to a circular staircase that went down.

At the bottom, they turned to their left and went back under the huge room well above and were stopped by a big glass wall in front of them. Peering through, Javor could see that at this level what lay ahead was the actual spillway and the turbine that spun accordingly. It was tied via cables and arrays to the ceiling, and all were vibrating slightly.

Effram spread out his arm to encompass the whole room. "We have the six turbines all unpowered by the Boathi bombs which took them out, but the one that is running comes out of our extra or side spillway. The Boathi missed that one, and we push more than 150 MW of power out of here at a time. That adds big time to our power production here on Bones—we have many more plants—some in the north push 1000 MW of power in a day too.

Javor watched and thought on that for second or two. "So the dam creates power; it's pushed to the substation over at Adair, then via towers to the grid that runs over the continent. If that's the case—is there an Achilles' heel in this system?"

Effram nodded as he led them back to the circular staircase and started back up to the ground levels. "If anything—our weakness is the lines themselves. There are so few crews who can update the lines, change the lines and insulators, and when we have a nor'wester like a few days ago, how to fix the lines too. 'Til we can ramp up those crews and get them out there on a daily basis—our big area where we run into trouble is the line crews."

He opened the doorway back through the large generator room and toward his offices.

Back there, he asked an aide to help them use the

ham radio setup. Sue excused herself to talk to the Regime HQ and update them on their new mode of transport.

Two of the other dam workers provided a quick dinner, and they ate quickly. Sue got back in time to get the last sandwich.

"HQ says take it easy with the truck—they'd love to see it themselves. Oh, and in Lindos, we should not enter that free city with the truck they said, but park it outside of town like she's wrecked. Else, they said, we'd be targets for sure."

She smiled at Effram and rose. "We gotta go, I'd guess, but did want to say thanks! For the lunch and the quick tour too, Effram. Next time through, we'll stop again for sure."

A few minutes later, they were all back in the truck, and Bixby was happily ensconced in the middle of the back seat, looking out the windshield as Javor started her up and they waited for the gate to slide open.

As he slowly left the dam area, he turned to his left and the truck moved back up the slope of the road to head toward Adair. In the side mirror, the dam grew smaller as they went back toward the interstate.

"Anything else perhaps that the Regime had to say?" Wayne said from the back seat.

Sue nodded and turned to face back toward him.

"One thing of import, yes. That in the Badlands, there was a large uprising of some of the tribe there —and that meant that the interstate would be the only safe way through same—stay off the regionals, they said. Not important for us, as we're going to use the interstate, but good to know," she said and then reached back to ruffle Bixby's chest. The dog stretched out his muzzle to enjoy the scratching.

"We'll need to find a spot to camp out tonight," Bruce said.

They sat in silence as they thought about the trip ahead and what further issues would arise.

As the truck made its way along the regional roads, Wayne was still bitching from the crew cab area.

"If the dam bombs had fallen just a couple of miles to either side, she'd still be up and we'd be safer—hey, what the hell is that?" he suddenly added to his rambling complaint as he pointed off to one side of the road.

After leaving Adair and getting back up on the interstate, they'd not gone more than ten miles when they saw that the interstate roadway had fallen.

"That was probably due to the large town below," Sue said. "Used to be a bedroom

community for Lindos, "which is like only about
forty more miles away. Trains, as I remember, were
big here—commuters would go in and out daily.
But the Boathi took care of that, and the interstate
was a bystander that got caught in the bombing.
Most likely, 'cause the railway yards here were so
big ..." She pointed to the massive craters and
twisted rails ahead.

They had left the interstate by doubling back
about three miles to an on-ramp, and taking it
down, Javor had turned the truck around and
headed back east. This regional road, a four-lane
road, had few cars or vehicle pileups, and they
made good time until they found their way ahead
blocked.

The interstate itself had fallen down ahead, and
its six lanes of concrete, re-bar, and twisted beams
lay ahead and completely blocked the road itself. A
large crater on the right of the roadside stretched
outward to the right, and there was no way to guide
the truck that way.

Sue pointed to the left and said, "Try the left—
slow though, I'd think."

Javor had the same opinion and nodded. He
backed the truck up a few yards, spun the wheel to
the left, mounted the curb, and went over onto the
overgrown weeds and pockets of trash and debris
from the interstate. Twice, they all had to get out

and manhandle something out of the way. The biggest thing they moved was a beam. They hooked the beam up to the back of the truck using a chain they found in the truck and yanked the beam just a few feet to the right. As they slowly made progress, Sue spoke up finally.

"We need to camp out somewhere, so let's look for that spot first and worry about getting by all of this tomorrow, shall we?" and that got nods from them all.

Javor slowly took the truck to the left as far as he could, right up beside a small slope. The banks of the slope climbed up the side of one of the interstate support pillars and slowly went ahead. From what he could see, the slope went well past the pillar itself, and that might give them some cover on one side of the truck.

He slowed and looked at Sue.

"With the slope, we're covered on that side. All we need do is to have our eyes on the other sides and we'd be fine, I'd think."

Sue held up a finger and got out of the truck. The rest of them followed her.

Javor watched Bixby carefully. Bixby loped along ahead a bit, then climbed the slope to dig for a moment, and then came back to the group who were peering around the parked truck.

Slope on the left side. Ahead, overgrowth and

what looked like a small dip down a culvert of some kind. To the right was the pile of interstate rubble that ran on for hundreds of yards. Huge beams now showing the oxides of rust and twisted sections of concrete and re-bar lay like broken crackers in a box. From where they were now, they couldn't see where the interstate was back up and they'd be able to use it again. Right now, they were stuck on the grade-level regional roads, which as they'd heard from the Regime could be a problem.

They all looked at each other and then shrugged en masse.

"Not a problem, I think." Sue smiled.

"Bruce, your turn for first sentry duty 'til say midnight—Wayne 'til four and then wake me up. We've got some food in hand as well as boxes of whatever kind of food stuff Nutty was carrying to Walkerville. Let's all try to find a spot to sleep—dibs on the front seat of the truck. Back though would be great too, I'm thinking." She went back to the truck as did Javor, and he turned Nutty off and then grabbed his pack from the rear of the truck.

With one of the guys taking the crew cab seat, he decided to sleep on the top of the truck, rather than in the back. Don't have claustrophobia, but being out in the open is always better. Might be a bit safer too. Course, how the hell do I get Bixby—wait, he thought.

He went to the back end of the truck and slowly climbed the slope, finding handholds with the weeds and enough space to force a foot up and up again. As he got to about the height of the truck, he stopped and looked back—and the top of the truck was only five feet away. He grinned as Bixby stopped whining, scrambled up beside him, leapt over that gap, and strutted around on top of the truck.

Not a problem, Javor thought as he went back down and got his shotgun and backpack too. Removing two MREs that he'd stocked from the Drake, he also got a fresh supply of jerky bars and tucked them into his armor vest pocket too.

Back down on the ground, Sue and the others were sitting on debris from the interstate. The twisted concrete that Bruce was on looked almost like a love seat, and he stretched out his legs and sighed.

"Wish we could have a fire—but yeah, I know, not safe. Wish we all had some beers and music too —if I gotta be in the woods, I'd like more to do," he said wistfully.

Wayne nodded. "How unlike you, Bruce, to want what we can't have. Just don't get too comfy on that loveseat you're on—sentry duty means staying awake, eh?" he said, and while he meant to josh with Bruce, one could tell he meant it.

Sue looked up from the packages of the Nutty Spread that she was carefully layering on top of some kind of cheese. She waited until she'd gobbled down a big piece before she spoke.

"Sentry duty Bruce is good at—hate to think you'd get by him. But yeah, we are in some kind of zone that the Regime said we shouldn't be … so let's all pay close attention to anything that seems like it could be trouble.

From above them on top of the truck still, Bixby suddenly barked and wheeled around. They could hear him scrambling down the slope of the embankment, and it sounded like an avalanche as he was in a hurry, and Javor picked up his shotgun just in case.

The dog went right by them and off into the debris field from the fallen interstate, and they could hear him barking. Sue motioned for them all to spread out as they turned to face outward.

Bixby stopped his barking and growled now instead. Something else growled back, and Javor was off at a run.

He moved over some of the piles of concrete and when he reached a small cleared spot, he stopped cold.

Bixby was backed against a tall pile of rubble, but what faced him was a creature Javor had never seen before. More than five feet tall at the top of its head, it was, or should have been, pure white fur—but the animal was so dirty that the word white would never be used to describe it's color. Big head, fangs that were bared, and it looked like a cross between a cat and something else. Claws flexed out of the muddy fur around the feline's feet, and the tail was held back but flicking from side to side—a hunting gesture he knew from other cats.

Javor had no idea what the other animal was, but as he aimed his gun, Bruce beside him said, "No let me—clean kill shot is easier with a rifle" as he pointed his rifle at the predator.

Bixby barked and barked, and then the sound of the rifle rang out.

The cat-like animal fell in a heap, twitching for a moment and then lying still.

Bixby went right up to it, ignoring Javor's commands to stay back and wait, and he sniffed the animal.

"Zoos here those years ago freed all their animals —including, I'd guess, this one, called a Kellas— dunno why though. Bigger than I remember from trips to the Arlington Zoo thirty years ago and more. Still, would have loved to have eaten Bixby or us! Good shooting, Bruce," Sue said as she turned to walk back to the truck and their meal.

Javor nodded. A Kellas, she'd called it. Big enough—almost twice the size of Bixby—to have eaten us all.

Calling Bixby did no good, and he had to grab the dog by the scruff of his neck to drag him back to their truck. He praised the dog though, reminding himself that if the Kellas had had more time, it might have not ended up so good for Bixby and them.

As they retraced their steps away from the cat, Javor looked up. It was growing darker as dusk was just about over, and a few stars could be seen in the eastern sky to their right. The shadows had deepened and the faint glow off the top of the slope behind them and to the west was almost gone.

Sitting once again on the same log, he had a couple of mouthfuls of his MRE—Beef Sloppy Joes the label read—and he noted that Bixby now had eyes for only him and the food.

He grinned at his dog and then pulled the rip tab on the second MRE. Putting it down, he opened it with his knife, and Bixby stared at him. Well trained, he thought, as he nodded toward the food and said, "Okay, boy, chow down, lad," and the dog wolfed down the whole MRE in a few seconds flat, chomping his lips together afterward to gather any of the gravy or drippings that were on his muzzle.

Wayne had watched the whole thing, and as he ate his dinner, he spoke up.

"A Kellas that attacks not at a good time for same
—just dusk now—instead of in the middle of the
night when hunting for a cat is always better might
mean something, eh?"

Sue looked at him as she wiped off some of the
Nutty Spread off her lips.

"Meaning?" she said.

"Well, predators—especially I'd think this Kellas
—would know that their success rate goes way up
when it's dark. So something made her approach us
in the daytime. She didn't even know that Bixby
was here—he was up on top of the truck. So
something else is making her pick a bad time—she
was after us—right?"

Javor thought this made sense and as nicely as he
could, he said, "Wonder what might prompt that
kind of a change in behavior?"

"No idea," Sue said, "but dusk it is, and I'm
bedding down. Bruce, you're up 'til midnight …
night, all," she said, and taking her things, she went
back to the front seat of the truck.

Wayne went too and Javor hustled Bixby along
with him, said "Night," and left Bruce alone in his
love seat.

Up the slope was a bit easier this second time,
and when he turned to jump across the gap, Bixby
was already there, lying beside his backpack.

Getting comfortable was a problem as no truck

roof was made to be comfy on, but his roll-out pad helped a bit. The foil blanket would keep him warm as it insulated him from the cooler night airs, and Bixby lay just an arm's length away on one side. He took off his armor vest and rolled it up around the Colt to use as his pillow. Only his shotgun was closer. The moons above were gently golden tonight as the last parts of their crescents were just slivers.

As he drifted off, Javor flexed his knee a few times. The alien tissue had surely done its job earlier in the day. But those kinds of demands on it usually meant that he limped for a few days. He just hoped that the few days were all it was going to cost him.

He smiled at no one and thought of home, his brother whom he hadn't seen now in almost a dozen years, of another dog he'd had when he was a youngster named Skippy, and how much fun it had been to be a kid.

He slept.

Dreamless sleep at first, and then the twenty years of decathlon training and what that had cost him in relationships and body parts came too, but tonight not so much. In his dream, he was training for the discus throw and the circles were so hard to grasp at first. It had taken him almost five full years to learn the proper spin technique.

How hard it had been to learn that the one-and-one-half spins were all to be phased in in sections.

His coach yelled at him time and time again that if he were just to focus on rhythm, it would bring about the consistency to get in the right positions that many throwers lacked.

"Executing a sound discus throw with solid technique required perfect balance," Coach yelled at him.

This was due to the throw being a linear movement combined with a one and a half rotation and an implement at the end of one arm, his coach drilled into him time and time again, and tonight's dream was no different.

As he squatted once again at the back of the circle, ready to spin counter-clockwise, he was pulled from his dream.

Something was wrong.

He felt that more than anything, as one hand crept out of the foil blanket and found the shotgun, and then he heard Bixby's low growl. Trying to get the dog to quiet was not possible, and Bixby jumped off the truck top back to the slope. Javor heard Bixby barking like mad as the dog crashed down the slope.

Something was going on, and he quickly got up on his knees as quietly as he could to peer around in the nighttime blackness as Bixby's frantic barking continued.

Big sounds like footsteps came from below in front of the truck, so he went back on his belly to crawl right up to the front edge of the roof above the cab below.

Something was moving toward the truck, and yet he couldn't see squat.

"No way around this," he said to himself, as he banged the butt of the shotgun down and slammed it into the metal roof of the cab.

"Sue—turn on the truck's lights," he barked out. As he brought the shotgun up to cover the front area, his eyes widened.

From behind him, a club cracked into his skull, and he lost consciousness in a sea of blackness and dog barks.

CHAPTER EIGHT

As the fog cleared when Javor slowly came to, he realized someone had gone through his clothing and his backpack. The first thing he saw was everything from his backpack in a jumbled mess across the top of the truck.

He shook his head and a foot nudged him. A huge club swung from the belt of the figure standing above him.

That foot was attached to a big solid man about thirty years old. He held a bow with the arrow nocked but just pointing at him, and he gestured with his head for Javor to get off the top and down the slope to join the others.

Javor did, but he did so slowly as his head was splitting. As he looked around the truck top, he couldn't see his shotgun. That was a problem, but he slowly made his way to the edge of the truck and leapt across the few feet to the slope. Too groggy to stand, he used his rear end to slowly slide down the dirt slope, and when he reached grade level, he tried to stand.

He hoped he'd never have to do again. Both temples began to pulse and a sharp pain shot down the back of his head too. That guy wields a pretty good club. He gritted his teeth as he made his way around the truck and over to the group.

Sue was nursing a hit that would blacken her left eye—if not the whole left side of her face.

Bruce, who'd been on guard duty, had taken an arrow to his shoulder. He pressed a rag into the spot all around the protruding arrow and grimaced.

Wayne lay still unconscious in a heap. Javor went over to him to straighten up his legs and saw no wounds. Club maybe, he thought.

And Bixby. Bixby sat quietly, beside another robed person who appeared to be the head of the attackers, and his tongue hung out as he breathed heavily.

"I am Disciple Anqas—I lead this team of raiders from the Forest Empire. You have a tablet. A tablet of ours—that you found when you found Khuno," he said as he pointed down at Bixby. "His master would have had it with him in his bag. You have it now. We want it now—and you can all live. Who speaks for you?" he finished as he looked at Javor and Bruce.

"I do," said Sue, "and what would make you think that we have any kind of tablet? Let alone one from Bixby's owner?"

The fact that a woman was in charge appeared to make the robed leader step back and think for a second.

"A woman leads ... that is so very different. But we have seen many things in the past hundreds of miles that have surprised us greatly. So, leader—do you have a name?" the man asked.

Javor thought he detected a bit of civility in the man. Of course, being held by six other robed men, all with arrows nocked and pointed directly at his group might have made him think that, he guessed.

"My name is Sue—Sue of the Regime—I run this cadre for them. Who are you and this Forest Empire?" she said as she stalled for time.

Javor carefully leaned forward over Wayne and patted him on the face gently. No response yet, but the robed men allowed him to find a canteen and wet the unconscious man's lips.

"We are the nation that is in power in the north— well north of this area. We know that the God who came and made all the changes to Ceti4 did so to rid the lands of non-believers. We await their return as our saviors and know that in the meantime we need to be as pure as we can. Of course, as you can see," he said as he pointed at Wayne and Bruce, "when people resist, they will need to learn that the Empire is the rightful new nation on Ceti4. The tablet is ..." he said.

Back on point, and he wondered what Sue would do, but she just nodded and then asked if they'd let her go into her backpack in the front seat of the car, to which he replied, "No."

Disciple Anqas nodded to one of the others to go, and in a moment, he was back with the backpack. After rifling through it, he nodded as he pulled out that tablet and handed it to Anqas.

He took the tablet, turned it on, and then scratched his head.

"Disciple Kaspi's PIN is his birthday too?"

The large robed man who stood over Javor nodded as he said "ten, twenty, seventy-two."

After Disciple Anqas keyed that PIN in, the tablet appeared to light up, and he was in. Nodding, he turned it off and then looked back at Sue.

"Just how far have you come for that thing? And boy, you guys must be fast," she said.

That got a nod from one of the bow holders who said, "More than five hundred miles in less than ten days ..."

Anqas frowned and waved his hand to quiet the

others. He stood there and stared at the cadre.

A woman with a face that was bruising down the whole left-hand side, a man with an arrow still in his shoulder, another with what could only be a screaming headache, and one that was still unconscious—hardly a group to worry about.

They'd never match the disciples on their return trip home; they'd most likely not even get past Lindos, a city where one needed safety in numbers.

"This dog-Khuno—who is the dog's master here?" he asked.

Javor looked at the disciple and smiled. "I saved the dog's life a few months back, and he's been at my side since. I take it he's no use to the Forest Empire—so I'd ask that you leave him with me—kinda like having him around.

Anqas stared back. For a full minute, no one else spoke and then he answered. "I will grant you the dog—Khuno. You will be his new master—do treat him right—we Disciples love our dogs."

With that settled, he said something to the dog. Bixby looked up at him, barked, and then trotted over to sit beside Javor. He licked Javor's left hand, his tongue making big sloppy paths across the back of Javor hand, and he paid no more attention to the disciples at all.

Anqas nodded and then he said to one of the bowmen, "Pick up all their weapons—we're taking them with us. We will leave you alive, but unarmed. You will not follow us or you will never even feel the arrows. You can go your own way — but a caution. The Forest Empire considers your word as our hostages — surrendering to save your own lives — as paramount. Do you all so swear?"

He looked at each and got a nod or a yes from the three conscious members of the cadre.

"The one asleep we will hold to the same standards. Remember your word," he finished, and in less than a minute, he and the other six were gone, dancing away into the darkness that lay off to the west.

Sue held up a hand and pointed to Wayne, digging in her backpack for the first aid kit.

After a quick look at Bruce and the arrow, she grinned at him and said, "You know the drill, Brucie ... on three."

She got in position directly in front of him, one knee above the arrow and one knee below.

Bruce squirmed and nodded.

"One ... two —" she said, and she yanked the arrow out a full count earlier, and he screamed loudly.

She looked closely at the point — no real barbs to speak of, yet she knew that would hurt a lot. She dug into the first aid kit, found a small bottle, popped the top off it, and sprinkled the powder down and into the wound. She took another small case out and reached inside for an injection stylus. She jammed it into Bruce's bicep and made sure that he got the whole dose. One more time she reached into the kit, and she pulled out a sterile dressing that adhered itself on his shoulder. She patted him on the face.

"Three, eh?" Bruce said as he leaned back to rest.

"Next time, it'll be three," Sue said, and that at least got a smile from him.

A quick thought struck Javor, and he groaned but went back up the slope to retrieve his things and bring them down to the area that was lit up by the truck.

"They missed my Colt," he said.

Bruce nodded as he added, "My small pistol is still in my ankle holster too. But they did get that beautiful new rifle I so loved."

Javor dug into the remains of what had been in his bag and pulled out a drone ball. He slowly twisted the top in a counter-clockwise direction. As it lit up, he pressed a button down deeply and said, "AI Nine-oh-one?"

The drone ball chimed.

"I want you to go west 'til you find seven bodies moving as a team. I want you to follow them at maximum height so you will not be found. You will radio to the other drone I have, AI nine-oh-two, your location and rate of travel at the end of each day. Understood?"

The drone ball chimed again.

"You are less than five minutes behind this group, so get going," he said as he then carefully looked up and tossed the ball into the air.

It went up, held its place for a moment, and then spun and rose as it headed west.

"Forgot I even took a couple of these off the Drake," he said to the open-mouthed stares from Bruce and Sue.

"Accurate?" Sue asked.

"Fairly, we've used them to track animal migrations, predators, and even divisions of marines on one planet. Long as she finds them, we're okay," he said.

"Range, Javor—if that guy was right and it's like 500 miles ... can we get that recon data?" Sue asked.

He nodded just as Wayne groaned out loud and grabbed his head with both hands.

Someone like the guy who clubbed me must have given him even a harder smack, but with my headache, I wonder how that's possible.

Wayne tried to slowly lift up, and Bruce held him down with his one good hand.

"Later, soldier. Just take it easy. Sue, got any of those headache pills?" he asked as he held out his hand.

Javor's hand joined his, and they all took a couple of the pills.

"So where are we? What and who are these Forest Empire disciples, and where do they fit in with the Regime? I thought you'd said that the Regime was the only real power left on Bones," Javor said as he settled back to lean against his backpack.

Sue had pulled out a small mirror from the first aid kit, but after a single glance at her face, she just sighed and put it back.

"Right—the Forest Empire is the power in the north—and that's all there is to it. For some reason, after the Boathi bombed our power dams and grid and then followed up with the virus bombs, all the people of Forest—as it used to be called—found God—the Boathi. For some reason, they think the enemy will come back, and so they all try to lead pious righteous lives. Least that's what they say. While they took away our weapons, they use bows and arrows and spears only—seen some of them toss a spear hundreds of yards too," she added.

Javor doubted that as he figured that Sue was just exaggerating for him, but he nodded.

"One thing though to remember—they are different than us. They look at life here on Bones— what they still call Ceti4—as a sacred trust between

236

each one of them and god—the Boathi. I've often wished they'd just come back and put a big one down on those two Empire pyramids they have in the middle of Forest, the capital. It is more than—"

She cocked her head to the side.

"My own tech skills are somewhat limited, but something just struck me. They said they'd been on the road for the tablet for ten days. Where was the tablet ten days ago?"

"Back in Maxwell," Wayne answered.

"Yet they found us here—on a regional road under the interstate. Would that not mean that perhaps that tablet was talking to some kind of Forest Empire network? While I like serendipity, I don't think that they stumbled upon us ..."

Javor nodded. That made sense. If the tablet was hooked up to a network, then it could be found. Like this one had been.

But there was no network he'd been told on Bones—the Boathi had taken care of all the planet's satellites more than eight years ago.

There were some important issues here, and Sue nodded at him too. She got it and she looked up at the eastern sky.

"Still nighttime. Let's just camp out right here— little less comfortable, but we're all used to that. I'll take first duty, Javor, and I'll wake you at four hundred hours. Bruce, Wayne, get some sleep lads.

As Javor tucked the pad down around him in the dry overgrown area at the front of the truck, Sue turned the truck lights off and the night turned pitch black.

A few minutes later, Wayne's voice rang out. "The lights on the truck were on. They know that, but they never asked about the truck or wondered why we picked this spot to camp out ... that's a bit strange, eh?" he asked.

There were no answers, but Javor nodded to himself.

Finding a society that would move five hundred miles in ten days and not even consider that a truck was alive seemed odd. The headache pills kicked in, and he drifted off into sleep.

In the fullness of the bright dawn sunlight, Javor rolled over and Bixby barely moved beside him.

His head hurt.

His one non-alien knee hurt.

His pride hurt too—he'd been surprised by a club-wielding goon, and it had cost him his combat shotgun too.

He slowly opened his eyes and saw just ahead of him that Bruce was still asleep.

He sat up gingerly and Bixby gave him an eye as

he slowly turned back toward the front of the truck. Sue was up and had a campfire going. He raised an eyebrow.

"The hell with anyone who comes over to see what we're cooking up—I'll plug them before they even smell our brekkie," she said.

In the pan that she'd balanced on three rocks sat a big mess of eggs—well, that's what the MRE package read along with just add water, squeeze the bag a few times, and cook like normal.

His mind wandered as his day started. He looked back at Bixby who stared at him with that doggie look of hey, where's my brekkie, and he grinned at his dog. Khuno, they'd said his name was, but he knew that Bixby already responded to his new name, so he'd never use it himself. He worried open the zipper on his pack and dug down until he found the kibble bag. He took out two full handfuls and laid them on a rock right beside Bixby, who didn't even bother to get up, ate it while still lying down. He then found that collapsible bowl, poured in a cupful and a half of water from his canteen, and added it to the rock. Whatever Bixby didn't drink down, he'd just add back to the canteen. "We share," he said to himself, and he smiled slightly, but the ache in the back of his head was pinching.

He flexed once on each foot. He stretched out a leg ahead of him fully and performed a full deep knee bend, first the left and then the right. He did not bother this morning with any kind of cardio.

He pulled out his mirror to see if he could see the back of his head by using it and the steel dinner plate. No luck.

Sue had been watching and said, "Yeah, I'll look at that later for you, now come get some eggs,"

As he sat and scooped up a healthy portion, which tasted pretty good, Wayne came back from the woods and joined them.

As he pointed back behind them, he said, "Just don't go that way anyone." Everyone knew what he meant and that was fine with them.

Sue finished her eggs first, and using some water, she boiled off the dirty pan on the fire. Moments later, she was up and over at Javor's back. Using a flashlight and a fork, she parted the bloody patch of hair around the spot where the club had taken him out.

"Um ... not too bad. Broken skin that has a nice scab of dried blood on it to keep out any infection. I'd perhaps say we do nothing to this 'til tonight when we hit Arlington." Finished examining Javor's head, she went back to tend to her boiling pan.

Bruce said, "Tonight? Arlington? My reckoning is that it's like a hundred miles away anyways, without all the interstate issues we'd need to find and get on and off too. Tonight?"

Sue looked at him and smiled. "We have—least as far as I know—the only working vehicle we know of. And while it is just a few more miles than one hundred to Arlington via Lindos—if we cut Lindos off and go there straight via regionals, we can be there today. Maybe even by afternoon tea," she said.

Javor nodded.

Wayne brought up the issues with that plan. "But that will mean that we're on regional roads—exactly what we were told to avoid by Effram back at the dam. Some kind of tribal uprising or something? Seems like caution might be a better route than speed, to me."

Sue nodded to him too but held up a hand. "Normally, you know I'd never preach to chance this kind of route. But one thing that Effram never took into account—nor for that matter did we all—is that the truck is fast. So fast that by the time someone has thought about doing us some harm, we're by. Gone. Dust is all we'd leave. That and a reminder that in our whole experience on Bones, we've never found anyone who lay in wait for the next passing truck. Because there aren't any—except Nutty. Sounds like we could be having dinner tonight in a real live city—warm beds and hot baths all around."

Javor wondered what the real driving issue was with Sue, but she did make sense. No one lay in wait for the next truck. By the time they even heard Nutty going by, they'd be by. With no other vehicles to worry about, he could literally drive to this Arlington by lunchtime if the roads were clear.

He realized though that gas could be an issue, so he spoke up right away. "Listen, before we decide on any route, I'd better check the gas use so far ... so wait a few minutes."

He stood again, walked carefully around the truck to the driver's side, and got up and into the cab. Turning on the key was the first thing, and he did that and then looked down at the display dash.

Down in the bottom left-hand corner was the fuel gauge, and that red line now sat right above the marker that he thought showed that they'd already used about one-quarter of their fuel.

It had taken one-quarter of a tank to travel about eighty miles or so.

That meant the gas in the back would give them plenty of fuel too as Arlington had been reckoned to be only about seventy miles away. A few turns, some roads being impassable would be right too, so, yes, they could get to the Regime today.

He turned off the key, made sure the truck was off, and returned to the group.

"So far as I figure, we used about twenty-five

percent of the fuel in the truck to come this far. Means that if Arlington is about seventy miles away, we can be there today for sure with no fuel worries."

He didn't know what to think about Effram's warning that some tribe was having an uprising. If that was fraught with risk, it didn't sound like the cadre felt that it was a stopper.

He looked at them all and said, "So?"

Sue looked at Bruce, then Wayne, and then at him. "When we go—we go damn quick, but we cut the big corner and we're in Arlington today," she said as she tossed the remains of those eggs and the boiling water into the fire pit and scrubbed it out with a bunch of leaves.

Javor gathered up his own gear. Really miss my shotgun. Want that back, I really do. Maybe one day. As Bixby finished drinking, he checked the bowl. The dog had left half a cup, and Javor tilted it to his own lips and swallowed it down. Flinging the drops away, he collapsed the bowl, tucked all back in his backpack, and donned his armor vest with the Colt. He checked the draw—not a problem—and then the safety. It was on and he reached for his pack.

Bixby was staring at him, tongue hanging out.

He smiled and fished back into his pack for a few jerky bars, and stripping one of the covering, he first took a bite and then tossed it to the dog, who wolfed the whole thing down in three chomps.

He put his pack in the back of the truck, got Bixby up and in the middle of the rear crew cab seating, and moved up to the driver's seat himself. In about three more minutes, they were all in, and Sue said, "Home, please ... and step on it ..."

#####

Javor was happy with the regional highway system so far.

Built over generations, it crisscrossed the towns and various cities all over the country. Here in the area now called the Badlands, it was a normal two-lane blacktop road that still had its yellow line right down the middle. Even though it hadn't been maintained for the past eight years, it was still in pretty good shape because there'd been no traffic using it for those years. Overgrowth past the shoulders was bad, and in some areas, the gravel shoulders were mostly green as nature tried to recycle as much as it could. There were potholes here and there, some with standing weeds, but the truck roared right over them with no problems at all.

Regional 17, which they had seen on a sign, was the name of their route. They had driven through two towns so far, right down the main drag of one of them too, but the roadway had been pretty clear. In the last twenty miles, they'd averaged about thirty miles an hour.

Not a moment after that thought went through his brain, the way ahead was blocked with an enormous crash that must have had forty vehicles in it. Javor slowed and stopped right before the first burned vehicle. He got out and walked the left side of the shoulder first. It was blocked by a pickup truck that had been tipped over, and as there was a culvert up ahead, a guardrail blocked that way. He shook his head and then tried the right side of the road. He walked almost the entire length of the pileup until he saw that a semi lay on its side with the trailer blocking the whole shoulder right up to the tree lot at the side of the road.

"Not passable at all," he said.

Sue, who'd walked beside him, agreed. "So ... back to the last left, take it, then try to circle around this crash-up, and then get back onto Regional 17?" she asked.

"Aye, that's about the size of it," Javor said. "How far back was the last road though?" he asked.

Sue shrugged and said, "I have no idea."

He smiled and said, "Then let's get on the road, shall we?" He hopped back up into the truck. After backing up and making a five-point turn to get Nutty going backward, they were off.

It was almost four miles back to the first left-hand road off Regional 17, but the mileage wasn't the problem.

"Shit," Sue said as she grabbed onto the dash in front of her. "Bloody zombies ... dumb ones, but you can never tell."

And she was right. In front of the truck coming down all of the intersecting roads at this four-corner stop, zombies were tottering toward the sound of the truck. The fact that they were responding to the first pass-by of the truck from about fifteen minutes earlier wasn't the real issue. The fact that they were in front of the truck was.

Javor slowed and then said, "Hang on, team."

He goosed the accelerator pedal, and the truck zoomed forward toward the more than fifty zombies. As he got closer, he left the right-hand lane, went as far left as he could, and then swerved into a left-hand turn.

In doing so, he hit six or seven of the zombies who were mowed down like wheat stalks in a harvest. One must have been closer to the outside of the truck cab, as the truck bounced up and over his body, as the rear wheels rode over him.

And they were clear. Javor twisted the steering wheel, and the truck went over to ride right down the yellow mid-line.

"One way," Wayne said from the back crew cab

seat, and everyone chuckled.

Behind them, the zombies turned to stagger down this side road, and in the mirror, Javor could see that already some of the upright ones had noticed there were bodies on the ground and had turned to stoop and eat. He cringed inside but said nothing. The fact that the Boathi had a virus that killed most of the Ceti4 citizens was one thing; the fact that it turned some into zombies, because Javor thought their genes somehow kept them alive, was another.

Ahead, a sign on the right, still held up by one corner, read that it was three miles to Regional 21. Javor hoped that it would run northeast like Regional 17. In any event, it was the road they'd take.

"Something to remember," Bruce said from the back seat as he stroked Bixby lying between him and Wayne, "We went back. And the zombies were already trying to follow us down 17. So in future, going back may mean that we run into zombies ..."

He had captured and said that which all of them had thought to themselves.

And he was right. Zombies would respond to the sound of the truck, but the zombies were so slow, they'd be miles ahead all the time. But going back could mean troubles—a good thing to remember.

Regional 21 came up and Javor slowed the truck,

as there was a minor pileup ahead. Someone in a truck much like theirs had slid off the road on the left to smash into the gas station. When that truck had hit the pumps, it looked like there had been a big explosion, judging by the size of the crater the truck loomed over, hanging half-in and half-out of too. Up on the roof was a large bank of solar panels that someone had used for target practice.

Another gas station, kitty-corner to the cratered one, had a lineup of cars still in line but long ago abandoned too. No solar panels, he noted, but there had been a set of four large wind fans to generate power—again the victims of potshots. While Javor didn't know the brands like a Bones native would, he pointed out that the station might be worth a look, and he turned a bit to the right, slowed, and then stopped the truck half on their lot.

Not a zombie in sight, he noted, so he stepped down and went cautiously toward the gas station store right at the front of the building.

"Mind me asking why we're stopping here?" Sue asked.

He nodded. "Because in my haste to get out of the Motor Pool back in Walkerville, something I never thought of was oil. We need oil for the truck often—and they may have some right here—so let's check, okay?"

Sue nodded and went along for the walk. The

station store was a mess inside, of course, but a whole wall held what should have been cold drinks. Wall-to-wall cooler doors stood before them. The coolers had run until the power had gone, so anything within those coolers might have gone bad long ago. But depending on what was in the sealed bottle, eight years of sitting in the dark might not have meant the same degradation of product. He touched the glass and found it at room temperature before he pulled open one of the cooler doors.

The intense concentrated blast of rotting flesh hit him like a brick, and as he slammed the door shut, he turned and gagged. He stooped over against the now closed cooler door.

"Must have had some folks in there when the bombs came down," Sue said as she pinched her nose shut, her breath coming in and out of her mouth.

He gagged one more time, trying to keep those eggs still down, and he slowly stood.

"We all learned that one a while back, as folks, for some reason we don't know, figured that being in a cooler with its own AC could protect one from the virus. Didn't work, of course, and there are stories of hundreds being found in big food store coolers. Even ones that folks did power a bit past the Boathi with solar or wind power. Shame really, but AC in cooler isn't a closed system," she said as she was still shaking her head.

He slowly felt a bit better and left the coolers for the half-torn-down racks of store items. It took a minute but he found the plastic bottles, and there were at least a few that seemed right. He hadn't checked under the hood, but he figured a gas engine could use the 10W or 5W grade, and he grabbed three of each. One had a hole in it and leaked over his hand, so he dropped it and said, "We're good to go."

Back at the truck, he opened the rear and used a bungee cord in the bay to hold the five bottles against the wall. He closed it up, went to the front of the truck, and hopped in his seat. Smiling at the group, he started up Nutty. They slowly drove off the lot, turned north, and took Regional 21. Javor figured they'd go at least five miles, and by then, they should be past that huge pileup they had to find a way around on Regional 17...

The *Sophon* came out of FTL and the sub-alternate at the helm announced their next planet in their search pattern.

"Captain—this one is named Ceti4," he said with what might be called a non-smiling face on a reptile. His green skin was lying flat, all the scales horizontal, with the resulting message to all that saw him that he was compliant and obedient too.

The captain nodded and said, "Full planet scan from high orbit will be fine."

The sub-alternate knew that such a scan, if empty, would show that this was the eighth of their nine-planet search, which would then mean the human ship must lie on the final planet. Simple math, really, he thought, happy with himself.

He nodded, complied, and turned to get those tasks done.

From high orbit, the Boathi scans would be broad, but any powered sources would show up on their scans. Not, he knew, for small little power plants that might power a village or small town. But major hydro, coal-fired, nuclear, solar, wind, or tidal plants would show up easily. And one way he knew was to go to the dark night side of the planet and let simple lights show him visually. He moved the *Sophon* toward the terminator and set up the scans to show power-generating areas.

The ship cruised slowly in high orbit, taking an hour to go all around the nighttime side of the planet. There were some huge mountains and rivers with no dams at all, yet a couple did spark a note that they could be in existence, but there were no large light sources nearby. There was a desert that seemed to go on and on too, and not a single power source came from that entire large area.

Heavily forested northern areas too, but no lights. A district with many lakes had a basic sprinkling of power and matching lights, but it was very, very small, he noted.

He changed the gain on the scans and asked the filters to phase out the smaller power sources, and the view-screen on the bridge wall slowly rotated as the high orbit continued.

At the far edge of the northern continent, he swung the helm below the equator and yawed the helm to go back through the nighttime space over Ceti4. Again, forests, plains, and deserts too ... but few lights and only one mid-sized power source generating at a dam it seemed. He scratched his scales below one of his ear openings, and the scratch was loud in the quiet bridge. He stopped immediately as he knew that the captain was the only one who was supposed to be able to scratch on the bridge, and he jockeyed the helm a bit more north.

When the nighttime tour was over, the helm was once again yawed to the daytime side, and the Sophon moved back across the northern continent one more time.

The sub-alternate heard the captain scratching and smiled but only to himself. He watched, as did the whole bridge crew, as the blue and green and brown continent below slid by, hundreds of miles at a time.

No real power could be seen. Yes, a few of the larger cities, some that had taken the Boathi bombs, he noted, appeared to have power coming from somewhere. And yes, there were some hydro power stations too, as well as a massive solar panel array out in the desert too.

But no nuclear meant that there was no human ship either. All ships were powered by some kind of nuclear reactor—that was the basic science that the Boathi had learned from the war with the humans. No ship.

"Scans showing no human ship, correct, Sub-alternate?" the captain boomed out.

He turned and his tongue flicked out twice and he said, "Aye, Captain. No nuclear at all."

The captain nodded back and made a few presses on his captain's console. The screen on the bridge showed the search map of the worlds they had chosen to look at—and now there was only one more left.

"Helm, let's leave this Ceti4 and go on ... the last system please ..." he said as he scratched his scales below his collarbone area, and the scratching sounds were very loud.

"Captain's prerogative," the sub-alternate said to himself, and he made the course corrections to the *Sophon's* next port of call and said, "Ready to depart, Captain," and he got the good to go from him and hit the FTL button to leave Ceti4.

#####

Wayne said, "Slow down a bit, Javor," as the upcoming sign was again mostly off its pylons. He opened his window and stuck his head out. He was on the passenger side of the rear crew cab seat, and he said, "Slower ... a bit more," and then he yanked his head back in.

"Says that the town of Raleigh ahead has a regional that goes back to Regional 17—only six more miles too," and that got a smile from them all.

As the truck was moving along at a bit more than forty miles an hour, they covered the distance through the farmlands quite quickly, and the town of Raleigh came up in a small valley ahead.

It had the same as always main drag with the angle parking that Javor thought must be a rule here on Bones.

This town was big enough to have a real downtown movie theater—what a great asset that must have been in the past. Now it had a bunch of cars and pickups lined up in front. He wondered when the Boathi bombs might have come down here, but he had no way of checking on that. He propelled Nutty down the main drag avoiding the occasional vehicles that were in the way. Once, he had to climb the curb to force a path through, but after a few minutes, they sat at the only stoplight in town.

On the curb, the sign read Dermody Street, and it pointed off to the left. A sign just below that read to Regional 17.

"That's us," Sue said, and she aimed her forefinger to their left.

Javor turned and the truck cruised down the new street with a small commercial district first. He noted a few restaurants came first and then what looked like a library and a funeral home too. Bet they were busy, Javor thought and smiled.

They proceeded slowly at first, as the commercial areas changed to big houses that sat well back from the street. Posh area was the feeling that they all got. On some large grassy front lawns were burned hulks of cars, and in one case, a hearse too, which was something to not even take into consideration.

Ahead at an intersection, there was another gas station, and Javor slowed down as the huge fans on top of the building were still turning and sounded like they were running smoothly. He pulled over to the curb, turned off the truck, and listened.

"If those fans have been turning for, what, eight years, then they must have had no grease and maintenance either. Yet there they are ..." he said and that got a hesitation in all their faces.

He got out, took his Colt out, and whistled for

Bixby to join him. Moments later, he entered the open front door of the service station store and looked around. Bixby walked right over top of the broken glass and store fixtures that had been destroyed years ago. Old magazines, too, pop cans that had been smashed, and a whole rack of gum and cough drops were strewn across the floor. Bixby nosed them a bit and found something to chew on, and Javor hoped that it wasn't going to make the dog sick.

He went down an aisle and then back up another. No goods really were worth even a second look, and he made his way past the snack-bar area to the rear of the store. At the corner before he turned same, he slid along the last cold cooler door on his right and slowly pushed his head around the corner.

Ahead was a long hallway back to the washrooms.

It dawned on him that the cooler door had been cold.

He reached back with his left hand and placed it flat on the glass door. Cold. It was cold rather than room temperature. Cold meant it was getting power, probably from the wind turbine fans up on the roof. Cold meant that someone was using the power to run the cooler.

He yelled out to the rest of his group. "Hey, we got power here. Come on in."

He walked around the corner and up to the cooler door. He waited for Sue to be just behind him, and then he opened up the thick doors and clicked the light switch.

Inside was a cooler that was obviously looked after. There was a long table off to the right of the door with stacks of food items and drinks. There was an area too that held food items—same as the food items they'd already seen back at the Motor Pool building in Walkerville. A cot with blankets and a stack of what looked like jeans and sweaters was in the corner.

On the table was a large map of the area, which Javor wanted to take with him right away. It had small blue circles drawn about some of the towns locally. Others had a red circle, but there was no legend to let him know what the colors meant. Around Raleigh, the circle was blue. So, maybe blue meant okay?

There was something odd too. A hairdryer was plugged into a power bar on the table.

Maybe just odd to me, he thought as he pointed to the red hairdryer.

Sue nodded. "Hairdryer—must be a woman here among others maybe," she said as she pointed at the cases of beer in the corner.

He grinned. "We should liberate a case, yes?" and that got a resounding pair of yeses from Wayne and Bruce.

He hauled one off the top and put it up on his shoulder.

"I should take the hairdryer," Sue said as she combed her own short hair with a set of fingers, which got a laugh from them all.

They made their way back out of the cooler and the station too and were in the truck a few minutes later, chugging along Dermody Street toward Regional 17.

In three more miles, they turned right onto Regional 17 and were back on their way to Arlington...

CHAPTER NINE

Nutty was making good time, Javor thought, as they came up over a rise with a small four-corner intersection ahead.

"Zombies off to one side," Sue said as she pointed out to the right ahead.

Javor slowed the truck. Something had come through here earlier, they figured, and killed some.

Dead zombies get eaten, they all knew, and few of the twenty or so even raised their heads, blood and torn flesh dripped out of their mouths. The number of corpses couldn't be counted from the cab, but as no one offered to get out to take a body count, Javor drove on.

"Okay, thing is," Sue said, "bodies mean someone was here recently to kill some of those zombies. And we have no idea which way those killers went from the four corners."

That got a trio of nods.

Wayne spoke up.

"Then as we're going straight through on Regional 17, we gotta just hope that they were on that side road is all ..."

As he drove, Javor wondered *what kind of time had gone by since those zombies had been killed.*

He wondered as the farmlands stayed on either side of the road. Farms that once had been farmed, growing crops and helping to feed Bones. But now, they lay in anything but working order. Barns had been burned, outbuildings wrecked, and paddocks and corrals were missing boards and posts too. At some time in the past, livestock had been killed and butchered—the bones now lay in piles that anyone could see. Occasionally, a silo had fallen, and the grain from inside lay all about, rotting now and unusable as seed for a new crop.

Off to the left, coming up a rise in the road, there was a fire somewhere behind a barn as smoke was drifting up. That looked a bit suspicious, Javor thought. That also made him slow down to just twenty miles an hour, and he moved over to the farthest part of the road on the right side.

As Nutty cleared the top, they saw four vehicles in the ditches. The closest one, they could see, was a bright blue pickup truck that had been twisted off the road somehow on the other side. As Javor motored by same, he could see that the truck's tires were ripped with shards of the rubber hanging down over the rims. The truck had not a scratch on it. It was in pretty good shape except for the tires. It had been carrying something in cardboard cases, as the cardboard now lay flattened all over the road ahead like it'd flown out at speed and had been run over too.

A few yards farther down the road was a small compact type of car with its snout buried on this side of the road in the ditch. On the road itself, the asphalt had been gouged somehow by the car before it left the road.

Javor was now only going fifteen miles an hour as he approached the garbage and detritus of previous accidents all over the road.

As the truck crunched over some of the pieces of metal, plastic, glass, and those flattened cardboard cartons under the tires, the sounds of the front two tires exploding broke through the crunching noises.

Bam! Bam!

And the steering got suddenly more difficult and then the rear tires too both exploded.

Bam! Bam!

"Damn," Javor said as the truck lurched to the left, and without tires, it slowly drifted down into the deep ditch. As he jammed on the brakes, what

little of the rubber was left on the wheels gouged
the asphalt and the dirt, and Nutty tipped over on
her side.

Sue ended up on top of him, and she was cursing
as she slowly lifted herself back up onto the
passenger side. In the back crew cab seat, Bixby
was barking as both he and Bruce had ended up on
top of Wayne.

The driver side doors were within a couple of feet
of the ground, so Wayne opened up his door, and
Bixby scampered out, but Wayne was too big to fit.
With Bruce's help, they were able to clear
themselves out the passenger side door and were
soon joined by Sue and Javor too. Bixby was
looking at Javor with what he thought was a look of
how could you do this to us, and Sue nodded too.

"Was that some kind of booby trap?" she asked.

Wayne had gone back the few feet to the roadway
and had picked up a few of those flattened
cardboard cartons.

"Yup, sure was," he said, "what's called a spike
strip in some places. Course, this one is homemade
but good enough to end Nutty's days," he said, and
what he said was true. With no tires, Nutty
wouldn't be moving again.

Someone had put some of the cardboard,
accident detritus, and some such brown rotting
weeds as cover to try to hide the strip that had a

series of barbs pointing upward that would deflate any tires that rode over it. At speed, it would blow out all the tires, which often then meant the car or vehicle would spin off the road.

"That's enough, nonbelievers," a voice yelled out from above them in the left-hand ditch.

Standing there were a handful of men — rifles trained on them all. Two of them had their rifles up at their shoulders, aiming directly at Javor and at Sue just outside the passenger doorway. Three more had shotguns at their hips, pointing at Wayne and Bruce who were taken by surprise.

But the look of these ambushers was the most surprising thing.

Each was bald except for a topknot of long hair that was braided and hung down to mid-chest level. Each was naked to the waist with some kind of tattooing on their chests of various designs — stripes, animal silhouettes, and even lightning bolts. All were in assorted colors, but the overall hues were in reds of various tints. If the word tribe was used as a descriptor, Javor thought, then, yes, this was a tribe for sure, as he gazed at their brown leggings and boots.

He knew they could see his Colt and he was directly in their sights. He stood still, wondering what to do next.

Sue had a pistol and Bruce had one in his ankle

holster.

Except that they have us sighted in ...

The cadre group stood frozen, while the ones with shotguns collected Bruce and Wayne. Each was frisked and then one of the tribe whistled, and three women came running out of the farm to the left side of the road. Each was like the males—bald except for the topknot of long hair, each naked to the waist, wearing the same leggings and short boots too. Javor noted that the man who'd frisked Wayne had not checked his ankles, so they had one gun at least so far.

The women's breasts, Javor could see, were like those of women he'd met all over the human worlds —some big, some small. But each was covered again with the same kind of reddish tinted tattoos too. Between them, they carried a string of chains and shackles, and while they got Bruce and Wayne shackled to the chains, two more came to the cab of the truck.

He too was frisked, the Colt taken away, and then was shackled together with Sue, who also lost her pistol, to the string of chains.

One tribe member said something in a language that he didn't know, and the man shook his head.

"You have a dog, it appears—but he just turned and ran," he said, and Javor realized that Bixby had in fact deserted them. That made him wonder, but a yank on the chain brought him back into the present.

The leader motioned them all to go back down the road to the farm drive, then turn left, and slowly climb the driveway to the barn. At the barn, the door ahead opened by sliding off to one side. Another tribe woman dipped her head, and they went by into the barn.

The first thing they all noticed was lights hanging from the high rafters, some lit in the dimness of the very high structure, which meant they had power. There were tables and a whole hodge-podge of chairs at same, and some were holding tribe members who were eating while others were chatting. But all stopped when the newest captives appeared.

One of the tribe members rose and ambled over to look at them.

"Four more—well done, believers!"

That got an acknowledgment from all of their captors via a loud tribal yell of "Huzzah!" and the tribal man grunted.

"You belong now to the Red Tribe," he said with a degree of force in his voice.

He pointed at them all and went on.

"We will be on our way up to the Forest Empire outpost—not far really—so the walk will not help you all get in shape very much. Once there, you will be sold to them—they need fodder for their next games, and the prices are good right now. We will also take your truck too, not that I'm told it may run again. We thank you for this, as it is not every day that we in the Red Tribe find such value on the road. Even from the spike trap from years ago … who knew that there was even a truck still alive?"

He grinned at them and went on.

"Amal, add these to the master chain, and give them each a portion of the dinner. We need them to be in as good a shape as we can."

Another tribe member, a man, nodded to the two shotgun-wielding tribe members who still had them under cover, and he grabbed the end of the chain off the barn floor and walked toward the far wall. There, a woman, who looked like she was the guard person, unlocked a locked door, and then Javor entered the side room.

It was a long room, at least thirty feet long, and inside sat a dozen more captives.

Some men, some women—no children, Javor noted, and he watched as the man connected the end of their chain to the large ring that held together all the sub-chains. Then he left the room, and Javor could hear the guard locking the door.

As they'd been effectively closed off, he moved over to sit as close to his group as he could.

Someone spoke up and said, "Where you all from?"

It was a man in a camouflage set of clothes, and he looked like some kind of soldier. There were four of them all dressed the same, Javor noted, and the rest were civilians.

Sue half-smiled and said, "We're from Maxwell, on our way to Arlington ... 'til today that is."

The man nodded. "Know anything about this Forest Empire tribe or group? Or this one?" he asked.

Sue shook her head. No sense in providing intel unless you were sure of the advantages for yourself, and Javor squeezed Bruce's good arm at the same time.

Later, they ate the dinner—some kind of stew with a big chunk of bread across the top of the foil bowl that killed their hunger pretty well. As he ate, he looked at and finally caught Wayne's eye and then stared down at his left ankle, then back an Wayne, and then the ankle.

Wayne nodded and said as part of the dinner conversation about Lindos the free city, he shared that he too had heard that a free city was a spot to enjoy ... as long as one was armed.

Javor nodded. Bruce had somehow gotten his revolver back into his ankle holster.

They had a gun ... and hope ...

267

Crash Landing

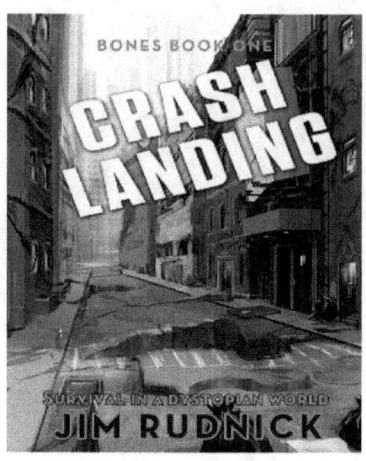

Dear Reader...

If you've made it this far, you're most likely thinking that this was the best SciFi you've ever read...

Or maybe not.

Maybe my ex-athlete Javor wasn't your cup of tea?

Or you hate the stupid Zombies and want them all to die?

269

Or does the Regime make your instinct's twitch with upcoming events?

So I'd like to ask you for a favor?

Would you mind taking a few minutes to write a review for me please?

And I'm talking honest too! Nothing makes us writers get better than book reviews!

Your comments help others know what to expect when they're looking for a great SciFi read...

If you want to write on any of my books, then just click one of the links below...

And thanks once again, I'm looking forward to reading your comments!

Jim Rudnick
2016

www.ingramcontent.com/pod-product-compliance
Lightning Source LLC
Chambersburg PA
CBHW070853250626
47159CB00003B/1052